Death
at
Bandit Creek

Praise for Amy Jo Fleming

Amy Jo Fleming "blows me away with her amazing, layered story. I know it will make a terrific addition to the Bandit Creek Series."
— CJ Carmichael, Romance and Intrigue Author

"What a ride. I was totally drawn in by this action-oriented story. Amy Jo Fleming is a master at weaving a plot."
— Suzanne Stengl, Romance Author

Death

at

Bandit Creek

A Bandit Creek Mystery

To Grant,

I hope you enjoy
my book.

Amy Jo Fleming

Amy Jo Fleming

Publisher: At The Keyboard Ltd.
Cover Design: April Martinez

www.AmyJoFleming.com

Acknowledgments

It Takes a Village

The whole Bandit Creek project was like nothing else I have experienced. Imagine 30 women and 1 man coming together to write a series of books set in Bandit Creek, Montana. Many thanks to Vivi Anna who came up with this brilliant idea. We had a wonderful community of writers who collaborated to produce this series.

So many people assisted me along the way including Suzanne Stengl, CJ Carmichael and Lawna Mackie and I want to thank each of them.

In the past few months, Rolf Stengl has done a complete re-read of my book and I want to acknowledge all of his hard work in making this a much better book.

Thank you all.

For David, Cat & Scott

Chapter One

Bandit Creek, Montana
October 18, 1911

Eileen McArthur knew she was in danger. She just didn't know why. An icy feeling crept along her shoulder blades. She could sense someone watching her from outside the classroom window, but every time she looked up, no one was there. The last student had left hours ago, but she was still agonizing over her letter. She had to finish it before she went home. The sun's last pale rays touched the tops of the mountains and it would get dark in the valley fast. After last night, she didn't want to walk home in the dark.

The letter finished, she looked for a place to hide it. She walked to the back of the classroom, pulled a few books from the bookcase and hid the letter behind David Copperfield. Tomorrow, at lunchtime, she would walk over to the post office and mail it. She said a brief prayer over the letter. Neil had to come and get her. He just had to.

She picked up a gold locket from her desk and made a quick decision. Back at the bookcase, she put the locket in with the letter. This time the book stuck out a little bit, but that was all the time she had.

She pulled her blue wool coat over her shirtwaist

and slid the matching hat on her head. Outside, a wind blew down off Crow Mountain. The cold cut through her coat. She shivered and a skittering noise behind her made her gasp. When she looked back, there was nothing to see.

Eileen boarded on the Dredger ranch outside of town. She had to walk down Main, past the cemetery and on towards the mine. The Dredger road branched off at a bend just outside of town, ran up a canyon, and ended in Deadman's Gap. Most days she walked to and from school with the three Dredger children. The walk passed quickly when she was with them, but tonight it seemed endless.

Ahead at the corner, in the lights of the Powder Horn Saloon, she could see Annie Hamilton, in her usual red dress, standing beside a window. Annie was talking to Luc Branigan. Luc was a respectable rancher, and Eileen didn't know why he would spend time with a prostitute.

No decent woman would meet Annie Hamilton on the street, and Eileen hurried across the road to avoid them. She heard the words Dredger and money, and saw them both look at her.

In the growing darkness, Eileen stumbled into Jack. He leaned against the wall, out of sight, watching what was happening on Main Street. Jack grabbed Eileen to prevent her from falling. Jack, or JD, usually carried a bottle of whiskey and was more often drunk than sober. She could smell the liquor on his breath.

"You don't want to be going this way," he mumbled.

"What are you talking about?"

"Don't let them catch you alone," he whispered.

Eileen shook loose from his grasp. Crazy old man. She hurried down the street away from him.

The clouds rolling in from the west were darker now than when she'd left the school. How could she have let it get so late?

Normally, she could have caught a ride to the Dredger place with Luc Branigan or one of his ranch hands, but after their run-in last week she wanted to avoid him.

The road curved past the cemetery. Poor folk were buried in this cemetery. Chinese miners, ranch hands, anyone without money, were buried here. Tree branches moaned in the wind. What an awful place to end up, Eileen thought.

And then she saw a light shining in the cemetery.

Who goes to a cemetery this late at night? This was a night to be at home in front of the fire, not out roaming in the graveyard.

Boots thudding softly on the road, Eileen went as fast as she could past the cemetery and around the bend. The light was moving and she could see it at the foot of the turnoff leading to the Dredger place.

Tommy Dredger stepped from behind a tree. Tommy was small for his six years. In the lamplight,

Eileen could barely make out his blond hair.

"My God, you scared me," she gasped. "You should have gone straight home after school with your sisters. What are you doing, moving through the trees like that?"

"I came to watch for you," he said.

"Why?" Eileen was surprised.

Tommy's eyes were wide. "I need to tell you that the bridge is blocked. A wagon from the mine spilled its load. Come around by the ford in the river. I'll show you the way."

Eileen peered down the road. The night was pitch black, not even the moon to light her way. She couldn't see the bridge. Tommy and his light moved along a path that ran beside the cemetery and then straight on to the Branigan ranch. She decided to go after him.

Eileen followed Tommy into a clearing. His light fell on a man, someone waiting for them.

"You're a good boy, Tommy. You go home now," the man said.

Eileen felt a hand on her arm.

"What about Miss McArthur?" Tommy asked.

"She and I need to do some talking. Remember, I told you, it's a secret." In the darkness, the boy held up his light.

"Are you sure?"

"Tommy, wait for me," she pleaded.

"You don't want to be frightening the child," the man said.

Eileen felt cold steel against her throat. She wondered if Tommy could see the gun in the darkness. Probably not. She watched the boy disappear into the night.

"Why are you doing this?" Eileen croaked.

Chapter Two

Alec Forrest was elected Sheriff of Bandit Creek in 1909, two years ago, when he was only twenty-three years old. Some people considered him too young for the job, but he was diligent. He was working in his office, a big fire burning in the stove, cozy despite the freezing weather, when Mrs. Ernest Miles marched in to see him. He was certain that his age was part of the reason that she felt it necessary to visit him so often. She sat down facing him from across his desk.

Mabel Miles was the minister's wife, and in a little town of 300 people she felt herself to be of some importance. Unfortunately, she was frequently here in his office telling him how to do his job.

"What can I help you with today, Mrs. Miles?"

"It's about the teacher, Miss McArthur." Mabel leaned forward. "She's missing, Sheriff. She's been missing for a week. Ever since the big storm. Nobody knows where she is."

After Mabel left, Alec put on his shearling jacket and turned up the collar. He pulled on a fur hat and leather gloves. His first stop was at the schoolhouse located on a hill above Main Street. It was unlocked, but that was not unusual. There was a pair of shoes under the teacher's desk and a leather manicure set in the drawer. He paged through the books on her desk. Her lesson book contained a lesson plan for October 19, the day after she had gone missing.

The next day, the sheriff rode out to Otto Dredger's ranch, but the teacher wasn't there. Otto was away, so the sheriff spoke to some of the ranch hands. They didn't know anything about the missing woman, so the sheriff knocked on the door of the farmhouse.

Otto's wife, Eliza, answered. Despite her loose clothing, Alec could see she was expecting a baby.

Eliza said that the teacher had not come home from school one day. It was totally unexpected and not at all like her.

"Miss McArthur usually walked home with the children," she told the sheriff, "but she sent them home on their own that day. And then she just didn't come home."

"Did she have a young man?"

"No, she just taught and then came home with the children. On Sunday, she would accompany me to church. She was a big help around here."

"What do you think happened to her? You must have some idea."

"I don't know what to make of it. And if she got lost in the storm . . ."

Alec headed back to town. Otto Dredger had

alerted the parents and the school board. The board were pretty sure she wasn't coming back and they had already hired a new teacher. Over the years, teachers had frequently left Bandit Creek, but Eileen McArthur was the first one who had simply disappeared with no warning.

The teacher hadn't bought a ticket for the train. She hadn't taken a stagecoach either, so she must be somewhere close by.

The following week, Alec spent his time questioning parents and neighbors, and riding out along the maze of mining roads and trails that cut towards Crow Mountain.

On the night of the teacher's disappearance, a storm had blown in, with heavy snow. Since then, the days had all been freezing and the snow lay deep on the ground. Today the sun was a white disk in the gray sky. Weak rays of sunshine filtered through the black spruces and naked aspens.

He was not sure that he was accomplishing anything, but riding was better than sitting in his office, waiting for something to happen. He couldn't believe that she would still be alive if she was lost out here.

Chapter Three

November 1, 1911
Kalamazoo, Michigan

The train depot in Kalamazoo was filled with people rushing to catch the train. Charlotte Fraser checked her blue trunk and watched it disappear. It held everything she owned and she wouldn't see it again until she reached Bandit Creek. She turned and walked with Mr. Sharp out onto the platform.

Charlotte did not feel like talking, she wanted to be on her way. Mr. Sharp looked puzzled and then he asked, "Are you sure you don't need any money, Charlotte?"

Charlotte still had some of the money he had lent her a year ago, to pay her tuition at Normal School. "No, Mr. Sharp. I owe you enough already." She added, "I don't know what to say. You and Mrs. Sharp have been so good to me, since my family went west."

"We both love you, Charlotte, you know that. So does Ora."

Charlotte smiled. "Ora will always be my best friend. No matter what."

"I wish you were staying for her wedding," Mr. Sharp said.

She patted her handbag. It held her contract with the Bandit Creek School Board. It was unusual to be starting in November, but the old teacher had left unexpectedly. Charlotte would earn the incredible sum of $800.00 to teach until June next year. "I need to start working, Mr. Sharp. I want to pay you back the money you lent me."

Charlotte gave Mr. Sharp a little hug. It was the first time she had ever touched him. He hugged her back.

"You and Mrs. Sharp have been like family to me. I can't tell you how much you mean to me."

He patted her arm again and she continued, "Thank you for everything."

Charlotte found a seat on the train. At seventeen, she was on her way to Montana, a place where she didn't know a soul.

Chapter Four

Luc Branigan spurred his horse, Rebel, out to the front of a herd of yearling steers, turning them down towards Bandit Creek.

Branigan's brother, Ty, and their cowhand, Dusty Lowe, tailed behind the steers, riding herd on any who lagged. They rode on Branigan land along Bandit Creek, on the ranch Luc and Ty had inherited from their father five years before.

Luc spotted some cow and calf pairs on a bluff near the creek. He gestured to Dusty who rode over to check on the cattle.

Dusty caught up to Luc to report. "The cows have our brand. The calves following them all have the Dredger brand."

Rage overcame Luc. "Dredger," he shouted, disgust in his voice. "Every spring he's out on the open range, putting his brand on every new calf he finds."

"What are we going to do, Boss?" Dusty asked.

"Time to eat," Luc said. "Start a fire and get the coffee going."

Lunch was a meal of biscuits and beans. After they finished, the three men sat around the fire, drinking their coffee.

"I can't let Dredger get away with this," Luc said.

"We should talk to the sheriff. Alec Forrest can

help." His brother, Ty, was ever hopeful.

"What's the point? Dredger is a big rancher with a host of cowboys working for him." Luc paused. "The sheriff can't help us."

"It's his job, Luc. Alec Forrest is a good man."

Luc shook his head. "Dredger will just say it's all a mistake. And the sheriff is barely more than a kid. We may never even find these calves again. No, we have to take care of this ourselves. Today."

Luc looked over at the two men. "Drive those calves over here, and tie them down."

He took a branding iron out of his bag, a large size running B, and settled it onto the remaining coals. When the iron turned ashen Luc took it out of the fire. He tested it on a nearby log.

Dusty cut the first calf away from its mother and drove it past Ty. Ty wrapped his lariat around the horn on his saddle. He roped the calf. Ty's horse held firm. Ty jumped off his horse and turned the calf. He wrapped the rope around the calf's legs and tied it down. Then Dusty joined him to hold the calf steady.

Luc carefully aligned his branding iron with Dredger's D and seared through the hair and the outer skin layer of the calf. When he was done, it left a mark the same color as the leather in his chaps, an even brown. They cut the calf loose. It got back on its feet and ran towards its mother.

After the fourth calf, Ty remarked, "Dredger will know he and his men branded these calves. When he comes looking for them, and sees our brand over his, there'll be hell to pay."

Luc didn't like trouble any more than his brother. "I did a pretty good job of lining the brands up," he said.

"We don't want a fight with Dredger, Luc."

Luc thought about Ty's words. Dredger had always caused trouble for their father and now he was stealing their calves. He turned to his brother. "We'll get these calves on the train out of Bandit Creek today. We'll take them along with the yearlings."

Ty muttered something.

"Don't worry, Ty," Luc assured him. "Dredger will never know what happened to these calves."

· · · · ·

Luc drove the cattle along a bluff above the river. Some ranchers liked to drive their animals right down the main street of Bandit Creek. Because they could. Because they liked to remind people that cattle had free run on unfenced land. Luc thought it was all just a show of pride, and not good for the cattle. It was a little farther along the bluff, but they would reach the railway calm and manageable.

The train station at Bandit Creek consisted of a two-story building with a waiting room, an agent's office and a freight room on the lower floor. Beside the main track were two sidings. Alongside one spur were some cattle pens and a loading chute.

Sam Wilberforce was the stationmaster and cattle agent. It was two o'clock when Luc strode into his office.

"Luc, I expected you earlier. The train goes out at four p.m."

"Sorry, Sam. We stopped to eat along the trail."

Sam sighed. "I need a bill of sale for your cattle."

"Right here." Luc handed the papers to the agent.

"Okay, drive them into the pens. I'll check them when they go past the gate."

Ty and Dusty drove the cattle into the yard. Sam sat on the fence to inspect them. Luc climbed up beside him. The four calves were mixed in with the yearling steers. When the second calf went past, Sam turned his head and looked at Luc.

"Luc, those calves were branded recently."

"We rounded up some mavericks as we came in. They were all following Branigan cows. They were ours, and we branded them."

"Stop that one for me," the agent directed. Luc called out to Ty who roped the calf. He pulled it on its side and tied it down. Sam dropped off the fence, went over, and looked at the brand. "This here calf was branded today."

"Yeah, they were following my cows."

Sam knew Branigan didn't produce as many cattle as the big spreads, but they were always healthy. They didn't leave cattle out on the open range to perish if there wasn't enough feed or the snow was too deep. They shipped well and sold for a premium back East.

After a few moments, Sam made his decision. "Luc, get these cattle loaded up in the train cars. I want them out of here this afternoon. And don't ever bring rebranded cattle to me again. I'm not taking sides between you and Dredger."

. . . . .

Otto Dredger pulled his Ford T truck up to the train station in Bandit Creek. He ran a hand over his hair. The blond waves touched his shoulders. Otto grabbed his hat from the seat beside him and put it on. The hat covered the fact that his hair was beginning to thin on the top of his head. Otto owned the biggest ranch in the valley, and always carried a gun, a silver-plated Colt Peacemaker. He checked the holster hidden under his long gray coat and slid the buckle over to ride on his hip. He liked to think of himself as a cowboy.

He could have sent one of his ranch hands to get this shipment, but he wanted to pick it up himself. It was that important to him.

He straightened his tie and went to look for Sam Wilberforce. Inside the station he asked the clerk, "Where's Wilberforce?"

"Out loading up some cattle."

Dredger wanted to deal with the man in charge, so he went outside and strode along the platform. Sam Wilberforce was across the tracks, watching some yearling steers and a few calves get loaded into cars.

Dredger eyed the cattle. They were in fine health. Wilberforce closed the gates on the last car, and then three cowboys emerged from behind the train. Dredger narrowed his eyes. Luc Branigan. Luc shook hands with the stationmaster, and rode off with his hands. Wilberforce turned to cross the tracks, then hesitated when he saw Dredger. That seemed odd.

Dredger waited for Wilberforce to get close enough for a little conversation. "Winter's come early, Sam."

"This wind is cold," Wilberforce replied.

"Them's some fine-looking cattle you loaded," Dredger continued, keeping his voice conversational.

"Yes, they were," Wilberforce said.

"All yearlings?" Dredger continued.

"All but four," Wilberforce said. "Are you looking for me, Otto?"

Dredger paused and looked again in the direction of Luc and his cowboys. He moved his head slowly, and then he turned his attention back to Wilberforce. "Did a shipment come in for me today?"

"Yes, it's here. I'll be glad to move it on out of

the warehouse."

There were two wooden boxes stamped with DuPont and the number 50 in big red print. The boxes were filled with dynamite.

"I'll help you get them loaded up in your truck. What do you need with a hundred pounds of dynamite?"

"I'm clearing some land. Dynamite is the best thing to blast those tree stumps out."

"Expensive, though."

"Cheaper than hiring men to dig them out. Better than burning them out. Especially after the big fire we had last year. Don't want to be starting another one."

The two men loaded the dynamite in to the wooden box at the back of Dredger's truck. Dredger brushed a few leaves off the open bench seat and stared in the direction of the cattle pens. The cattle had long been loaded and there was nothing to see.

Chapter Five

Sheriff Alec Forrest got to his office to find his deputy, Frank Waters, waiting for him with some messages. Some trouble had happened over at Lorelei's Cat House and Maggie O'Connor had a girl over at her boarding house who couldn't pay her bill.

The sheriff sighed. He sent Frank to check out the problem at Lorelei's and he went to see what was up at the boarding house.

The girl, Betty Parker, had a story he had heard too many times before. She had run away with a man. He left her in Bandit Creek at the boarding house. Betty was certain her man would be coming back for her, but she was out of money.

Maggie was insisting that the girl leave, and Maggie wanted to keep Betty's suitcase until she could pay her bill. Betty was scared. She didn't want to go back and face her parents, and she didn't want to leave the place where her boyfriend had left her. What if he came back and couldn't find her?

Alec learned where her parents lived, outside of Des Moines. He got Betty to leave when Maggie O'Connor promised to tell the boyfriend that Betty had gone home. Her bag and things weren't worth very much except to Betty and the bill wasn't that high. He got Maggie to relent and let the girl take her bag. In the end, Maggie was happy to see the sheriff take Betty off her hands.

Alec took the girl to the train station and bought her a ticket back to Des Moines. He told her that her parents could wire him the train fare, but he wouldn't be holding his breath for the money. He sent a telegram to her father, telling him to pick her up at the station in Des Moines. Finally, he took Betty out on the platform and watched her get on board the train.

He didn't really need the money. His parent's estate had been substantial and he had inherited the house he lived in from the old sheriff, Dan Wilson. He would far rather see the girl go home than run across her next week in one of Bandit Creek's saloons, working as a dance hall girl. Once the train pulled out of the station, he went back inside to wait for a few minutes. Not that he really thought she would get off the train, but girls in love… Sometimes they were too foolish for words.

There inside, standing beside a blue trunk, was yet another girl.

This one was especially pretty, with blond hair pulled back and blue eyes set in an elfin face. Did these girls just know where to find him? Was he going to have to buy her a ticket home, too?

• • • • •

Charlotte waited beside her trunk until almost everyone was gone. She was feeling lost and lonely. A tall man with a moustache strode briskly through the station. He wore a silver sheriff badge on his sheepskin jacket. He stopped abruptly.

Charlotte felt his eyes sweep over her. She raised her head a little and straightened her back. He was slightly alarming, but she wasn't going to let him know it.

The stationmaster came over to ask her who she was waiting for.

"Otto Dredger," she told him, "from the school board." The other man watched them intently.

"Are you the new schoolteacher?"

"Yes, I'm Charlotte Fraser" she said, standing as tall as she could.

"You hardly look old enough. Hope you'll be here longer than the last one."

"Otto Dredger was supposed to meet me here at the train."

"Otto was here earlier today. He's often down at the Powder Horn Saloon at the end of the day," the stationmaster said.

Charlotte looked at him doubtfully. "I can't go into a saloon."

The stationmaster wanted to close up. He gestured at the sheriff. "Alec, the teacher here, Miss Fraser, could use your assistance."

Now the sheriff looked annoyed. "Really, Mr. Wilberforce, did town council hire me as sheriff, just so I could escort young ladies?"

The stationmaster responded, "I'd take Miss Fraser to the saloon to get Otto, but my wife has her church meeting tonight and I've got to get home for dinner. Her trunk will be safe here in the station and I'll get someone to deliver it out to the Dredger place in the morning."

"That's fine, Sam. Go on home. I'll be sure Miss Fraser here gets out to Dredger's place."

The stationmaster tried to be friendly. "I've got two boys in the school. I hope you can teach them to read and such. Like I told you, Miss, we've been having trouble keeping teachers here."

The stationmaster locked up and the sheriff walked with her as far as a sign that read Sheriff's Office, a few buildings down the street. The sheriff became more casual. If it weren't for the badge he wore on his chest and the watchful nature of his eyes, Charlotte would have never believed he was a lawman.

"I need to stop in the office," he said to Charlotte. "It should only take a minute. I'll check on my deputy and then I'll take you down to the Powder Horn."

"Where is the Powder Horn?"

The sheriff pointed to a building on the other side of the road, with swinging doors and a wooden front. "Over there." She could make out the word Saloon painted above the door. Then he went inside his office, holding the door for her to follow.

Inside, the deputy, Frank Waters, was nursing a black eye and a cut to his left hand. "One of the girls in that fight had a knife, Alec, so I arrested her." Frank nodded towards the back of the office.

"Let me put a bandage on that cut," Alec said.

Charlotte gripped her purse and worried about how late it was getting. She would see if she could find Otto Dredger on her own. "I'll just go then," she said, and left before Alec could look up from Frank's hand.

· · · · ·

Charlotte made her way down the street to the Powder Horn Saloon. She stood outside the swinging doors waiting for someone to come out.

A woman in a loose-fitting red dress walked towards her. Charlotte marveled. The red satin was trimmed with black lace panels. She had never seen anything like it before. To her amazement, the woman turned to go into the saloon.

"Excuse me," Charlotte ventured.

The woman turned around and regarded her with an amused expression. "You know, respectable ladies don't usually speak to me."

Charlotte was taken aback. "Why not?"

"Because . . . oh it doesn't matter. What do you want?"

"I'm Charlotte Fraser. I'm looking for Otto

Dredger, from the school board. The sheriff said I could find him here."

"The new schoolteacher? How old are you anyways?" the woman asked.

Charlotte was never prepared for that question. Her mother could not remember what year Charlotte had been born and the church where she had been baptized had burnt down. With five children under six years old, her mother had sent her to school early. She knew she might be seventeen or even sixteen.

"Eighteen," she said, hoping to appear old enough to be a teacher.

"I'll see if he's in here." The woman pushed her way through the swinging doors. She turned back. "Better be careful around Otto. He likes to think he has a way with the women, and you're hardly more than a baby yourself."

The doors closed and the woman called out, "Otto, Otto Dredger, there's someone waiting outside for you."

Charlotte waited, but no one came out. The sun slipped behind the peaks and Charlotte felt a flicker of fear. What was she supposed to do, alone in Bandit Creek at night? It would be embarrassing to have to go and look for that sheriff again. After a few minutes, the woman in red came out the door with a brown-haired cowboy. "Otto Dredger's not here, Charlotte."

"He was supposed to meet me and take me out

to his ranch. What'll I do?"

"This here is Luc Branigan. He'll take you by the Dredger place."

The cowboy was thin and looked to be in his late twenties. He was wearing his chaps, like he had just gotten off his horse. "I hope it's not too much trouble," she said.

He jerked his head towards the general store on the corner. "I've got my wagon over at the store. It's loaded and ready to go," he said. "Dredger's place is next to my spread."

"Thanks for your help," Charlotte said to the woman in red. "I don't even know your name."

"It's Annie Hamilton, but it would be best for you to forget you ever met me."

Chapter Six

Luc and Charlotte settled in the wagon. "Where are you from?" he asked.

"I'm from St. Helen in Michigan. My parents had a farm there. I went to Normal School in Kalamazoo."

"You're a long way from home."

"My dad went out to California two years ago. My mom pulled up stakes after a year and went out to be with him. She took all my brothers and sisters but I've been boarding with friends since I started Normal School."

He gave her a surprised look. "Pretty little thing like you, I'm surprised you're on your own."

"I can take care of myself," she insisted.

"I only went to school to grade three," Luc confided as the wagon rolled down the road. "By then, I knew how to read and to do some adding and subtracting, so that was as much school as I ever needed. Been working on the ranch ever since."

Charlotte didn't know how to respond. This rough cowboy seemed nice enough, but her parents would never hear of a kid leaving school after grade three. Charlotte had gone up to grade eleven before Normal School.

"What do you do for fun, Miss Fraser?"

"I like to ride. I used to go to the movies in

Kalamazoo. I love to go to dances."

"Dances, now there's a thought. You, twirling to the music."

"I used to go dancing all the time, back in St. Helen. Or go to house parties. We would roll up the carpet so we could all dance."

"Going to dances," he teased. "Next thing you'll be telling me is you have a boyfriend back in Kalamazoo."

"I did have a boyfriend," she said. She thought for a moment about Gilbert. "Used to. But I don't anymore."

Luc took a minute to guide the horses around a corner. "Don't worry. You'll meet plenty of people here."

"I am sure I will." Her voice was quiet.

"There's a dance hall, the Atherton Pavilion. Every Friday and Saturday night, they have a dance."

"Do you go there, Mr. Branigan?"

"I go, but I don't do much dancing," he said laughing. "I'm a rancher, not a dancer."

Charlotte took in the town that was to be her new home. A pair of banks on the main street and an old log building with a sign that proclaimed it was the trading post.

"Who was that woman, the woman in red? Why did she say I should forget I met her?"

"Her name is Annie Hamilton. She is . . . she is . . . someone a schoolteacher shouldn't know.

That's just the way it is." Luc looked uncomfortable.

Suddenly it dawned on Charlotte. "Oh, she's a . . ." Charlotte couldn't say the word.

"Yes, that's exactly what she is," Luc agreed.

"She was so considerate. I can't believe it."

"Let me show you where the school is," Luc said, turning a corner.

"Is it near the Dredger place?" Charlotte asked.

"No, it's on a hill above town. The miners built this town right beside the creek, but it floods every spring. Especially the places set on the creek bed. The school's up higher, so it won't flood. The church is up there, too."

He pulled up on the horses. The school was two log cabins joined together by a covered breezeway. Long windows were cut into the log walls on either side of the door. The church sat beyond it.

"This is my first school," Charlotte whispered to herself. To Luc Branigan, she said, "Looks like there are two rooms. Is there another teacher?"

"No. The second part is the teacherage. But no one lives there. It's easier to board the teacher with a family."

"Why not with some family in town?"

"Why the teacher always boards at the Dredger place is beyond me, but Dredger is on the school board. He likes to throw his weight around."

They circled the buildings, took the main road back through town past the saloon, and past a cemetery. Around a curve in the road Luc slowed the wagon to take the turnoff to the Dredger place. They were soon lost in deep forest that encroached on both sides of the trail.

"Wouldn't want to meet anyone coming the other way," Luc commented as the team pulled the wagon around a curve.

"It's sure dark back in the woods like this," Charlotte said.

"Dredger built his house above his mining claim down on the creek. When the gold finished, he turned to ranching, and he didn't want to move the house. That's why he's back in the bush like this. Likes the quiet, I guess."

They turned into a yard. The low built house had a wide porch that extended the whole length of the building. Above the roof of the porch, three windows cut into the roof. There was a red barn in a cluster of some rough log sheds.

"Here's your new place, Miss Fraser."

Charlotte took some coins out of her purse and handed them to Luc. "Thank you for bringing me out here. I don't know what I would have done without your help."

Luc reached over and slid the coins into the pocket on Charlotte's coat. "It wasn't any problem for me to bring you out here. I enjoyed the company. Welcome to Bandit Creek."

Otto Dredger came out onto the porch. He was holding a rifle. He set it against the railing but made it clear he was ready for anything. "Branigan, what the hell are you doing on my place?" he demanded.

"Easy there, Dredger, I'm doing you a favor. I brought the teacher from town."

Mr. Dredger looked at Charlotte. "It's today that you came, was it? I got busy with some work. Well, you're here now."

He came over and offered his hand for her to climb down from the wagon. "Where are your bags?"

"My trunk is locked in the station. The stationmaster will send it out tomorrow."

"Looks like everything is taken care of."

Charlotte pulled her arm gently away from Mr. Dredger's grasp. She turned to Luc. "Thanks again for all your help."

"No problem." He touched the brim of his hat and favored her with a smile. "Hopefully, I'll see you again."

Mr. Dredger watched the wagon pull out of the yard, and Charlotte took the chance to have a look at him. He had long blond hair, with a narrow face and finely drawn features that were framed by a neatly groomed beard and moustache. He looked muscular enough, and he had the round build of a man who ate well. He was wearing a shirt and tie under his vest.

He turned to her. "You don't want to be having anything to do with Luc Branigan. He's trouble, for all his charming ways."

Mr. Dredger took a pocket watch from his vest.

"Just in time for dinner." He grasped her arm firmly and led her up the stairs. "Now come and meet Eliza and the family."

Chapter Seven

Annie Hamilton poured a glass of sherry for the pastor, Ernest Miles, and put the same amount of water in a glass for herself. It was almost eight o'clock on Tuesday night, the night the ladies' church group always met. As soon as his wife left for her meeting, the pastor would leave his house and make his way down the alley and up the backstairs to Annie's place.

Of all her clients, the pastor was her favorite. He was a thoughtful man who liked to relax and enjoy some sherry, forbidden at home, have a little conversation with Annie and then take care of his business. He would be gone within an hour, sure to be home before his wife got back.

The next man to appear on her backstairs was Otto Dredger. Dredger was not here for sex, but for information. He wanted a glass of whiskey, and she had a drink with him. It would steady her nerves. She didn't want to let him know how much she was afraid of him.

Dredger sipped his drink. He always took a while to get to the point.

"I saw the new schoolteacher came today," Annie commented.

Dredger did not respond.

"How is Tommy doing?" she asked.

"As well as can be expected. The children will be back in school, now that the new teacher is here. You'll be able to watch him come and go." From the balcony on the second floor of the Men's Club, Annie could see almost all of the comings and goings in Bandit Creek.

"I want to see Tommy," she said. "I haven't seen him in months." She tried to keep the pleading sound out of her voice. It would only annoy Dredger and make him more likely to refuse her.

Dredger ignored her. "What news did the good pastor have for you today?" Dredger asked. Finally, he was getting to the point of his call.

"Nothing at all. We talked about the Thanksgiving service coming up. I think he likes to practice bits of his sermons on me."

"Whatever for?"

"Grammar and such, I suppose. He hasn't forgotten I was the teacher here once."

"I don't forget either. I wish you wouldn't go on reminding me about it so."

"What do you mean, Otto?"

"You know, Annie, I feel responsible for the turns your life has taken. Sometimes it's just too much for me."

"I don't want to talk about it, Otto."

"Did he say anything more about Eileen McArthur?"

Annie felt guilty. Annie had told Dredger that Eileen had talked to the pastor. The teacher said that

Dredger had tried to kiss her. He'd been touching her, and then pressuring her not to tell anyone.

"I told you, Otto. The pastor didn't believe her."

"Are you sure he didn't believe her?"

"He told her that a good man like you would never harm a woman. He told her she just misunderstood what happened."

"Okay. Let me have another glass of whiskey." She filled his glass.

Otto took a few sips. "There's something I need you to find out."

She waited. He didn't say anything more, so she said again, "I want to see Tommy."

"Annie, I've told you. Eliza doesn't like it when you come out to the ranch. It makes her uncomfortable and she's going to have another baby any day now. I don't want her upset."

Annie bit her lip, helpless. "What do you want, Otto?"

"Next Saturday, when the miners come into town, there's something I want you to find out."

He set down his glass. "I've been waiting for Bill Ellis to pay me some money he owes me. I did some work on the road that runs past my place to the Ellis Mine."

Bill Ellis was the one of the owners of the Ellis Mine.

"So?" Annie asked.

"He keeps telling me he'll pay me when they bring the gold in from the mine. He's been paying the miners, but he hasn't brought any gold into town all summer."

"What do you need to know?" she asked.

"The date that they are bringing the gold into town."

"Bill Ellis doesn't come up here. What do you want me to do, ask every miner who comes in, when is your boss bringing his gold into town? That's ridiculous."

"Ridiculous?" he repeated her word.

She needed to watch the tone of her voice. She shook her head. "It's difficult, is all".

"Fine. Ask them when they'll be closing up for the winter. That will give me a pretty good guess about when they'll be bringing the gold in."

"I don't like this, Otto. What if those miners get suspicious when I'm asking questions?"

"You give them too much credit, Annie. Just do it and I'll see what I can do about arranging for you to see Tommy."

"Really?" she asked.

"Listen to me, Annie, my girl. On Saturday night, you find out from those miners when the mine is closing down. Come out to the ranch Sunday morning and tell me. And you can see the boy. Come while Eliza is at church and she'll never know."

Dredger left. Annie went out on her balcony to look at the sky. The stars were shimmering and she felt the burn of the whiskey in her throat. She remembered another evening. She'd had stars in her eyes back then, but the taste of the whiskey was the same. A few tears made a track across her cheeks. It bothered her how easily Dredger could manipulate her. Still, she would see Tommy.

. . . . .

Luc Branigan never bothered to come up the back way. He came through the Powder Horn Saloon and up through the doorway cut between the two buildings. Try as she might, every time she saw him, she had the same old feelings. The same old regrets for the girl she had been and the mistakes she had made.

"Dredger was here," he said. His hands were tight on her arms.

"I don't want to talk about it."

"You've been crying. Why do you let him come up here?"

It broke her heart to see the disapproval in his eyes. "I don't know myself, sometimes. Why are you here, Luc?"

"This is no life for you, Annie."

"I don't know why you bother coming here, Luc. I've told you, your money's no good here."

"Do you ever think I may care about you, Annie?"

"No, Luc, I don't." He had cared about her once,

but then she had betrayed them both. She remembered the look in his eyes when he learned about her and Dredger. Dredger, her mistake.

"Yes, Annie, I do. I care about you and I hate to see you living like this."

"That's why you used to drive all over the countryside with Eileen McArthur? That's why I see you with the new teacher?"

"Hell, Annie, you introduced me to Charlotte Fraser.

"Luc, it would be better if you just leave."

He gave her one final look and disappeared down the back stairs.

Chapter Eight

"Mr. Jack, you have to leave now. We're having school today." Charlotte shook the man awake. He smelled of alcohol and a half empty bottle of whiskey rolled on the floor under a desk.

The last thing Charlotte had expected to find in her schoolroom was an old drunk, but Tommy Dredger told her Jack slept there sometimes when it got cold. Once awake, he was a friendly drunk. He got to his feet and left her and Tommy in the classroom.

She sent Tommy outside to play, picked up the bottle and set it on her desk.

Charlotte looked around her classroom. Her very first classroom. There was a blackboard along two sides of the room. The wooden desks were set in careful rows with benches behind them where the children would sit. The teacher's desk was at the front. To her left, along the south wall was a row of windows that faced the mountains, away from the town. At the back of the room was a built in bookcase, filled with leather-bound books.

All those years of her childhood, playing school. This didn't feel very much different. She held out her arms and twirled around the front of the classroom. She might be a real teacher now, but she couldn't help herself. She picked up the chalk and wrote her name, Miss Fraser, on the blackboard. It was her very first school.

Charlotte sat down at the desk. The items on it were aligned just so and Charlotte thought it looked as if no one had touched Eileen McArthur's things since she left. Her charts and drawings were still on one wall.

Otto Dredger had told Charlotte that Eileen McArthur had only been at the school since the beginning of September and everyone thought she must have been unhappy. She simply left town one day.

Charlotte looked for the attendance book. She found a notebook filled with writing and began to read it—notes for each grade and each child in the grade. It was already past nine o'clock but the notes were going to be helpful. She felt like she was getting to know her students by reading them. Charlotte caught a whiff of perfume and felt the presence of Eileen McArthur watching over her.

It was past time for school to start. She picked up the whiskey bottle and jammed it behind some books in the bookcase at the back of the room. A letter fluttered to the floor. Charlotte looked behind the book and found a little gold locket. She stuck them both in her pocket.

She went outside and rang the bell. The children lined up in two rows, boys in one row and girls in the other, and filed into the school. They sat at their desks looking expectantly at her.

According to Eileen's journal, Dylan Branigan was not the oldest boy in school but he was the one most likely to get in trouble. Better get him busy right away. "Dylan, please go out and put up the flag."

She followed Dylan outside. Luc Branigan hardly looked old enough to have an eight-year-old son. "Is Luc Branigan your father, Dylan?"

"No, Miss Fraser. Luc's my brother. My dad died, back when I was small."

The children all watched through the window as Dylan raised the flag. When Dylan went back inside, he took the seat on the bench right beside Tommy Dredger.

Charlotte started the morning with the Pledge of Allegiance. The children faced the flag at the front of the class, and even the little ones knew to put their hands over their hearts. They began to recite the pledge.

"Take your seats, children. When I read your name out, I want you to stand up and tell me what grade you are in." Soon Charlotte had the children engaged in their first lesson for the day, writing math problems on the blackboard, making them increasingly harder for the older students.

At lunchtime, when the students were out playing, Charlotte went through the teacher's desk. Many of Eileen's teaching materials were there. So odd. Why wouldn't she have taken her things with her?

Tucked away at the back of a drawer was a little brass box. Inside, there was a framed picture of an elegant-looking young woman beside a man in a suit. The black and white picture had been lightly painted to add color to the faces and the clothes.

The woman was dressed in a blue coat with a matching dress. On her head, she wore an elegant hat trimmed with white feathers. She was holding a small bouquet of white flowers. Beside her was a man in a black suit. It was taken outside of a church and looked as if it might have been a wedding picture.

If this was a picture of Eileen, it couldn't be a wedding picture, of course, because Eileen was a teacher. Married women were never hired on as teachers. They were expected to stay home and take care of their husband and family.

There was also a bundle of letters. Charlotte didn't untie the ribbon that bound them together. The letters reminded her of the one she had found this morning.

Charlotte took the letter and the locket out of her pocket. She examined the locket, very pretty with a fine gold chain. The locket was worth a lot more than could be expected on the salary of a schoolteacher. Obviously, Eileen McArthur was a woman of some means. Inside the locket was the picture of a young girl. She was not the woman in the picture outside the church.

The letter was sealed and stamped, all ready to

mail. It was addressed to Neil McArthur. Was he waiting to hear from Eileen? Charlotte thought for a moment about opening the letter. It might solve the mystery of where Eileen McArthur had gone.

No, opening the letter wasn't the right thing to do. The right thing to do was to mail it. Eileen McArthur obviously wanted the letter to be sent if she went to all of the trouble of sealing and stamping it.

It was a fine day. Charlotte walked over to the post office and mailed it. It was the least she could do for the teacher who had left all her teaching materials behind for her.

Chapter Nine

When Charlotte got in from school that day, Eliza Dredger was down on her hands and knees going through a box she had pulled out from under the sofa. Her blond hair was drawn into a soft bun on the back of her head. She sat back on her knees when Charlotte came through the door and managed a tired smile. It was Charlotte's experience that women who were in a family way often looked radiant, but Eliza's face was creased with lines.

"Are you looking for something?" Charlotte asked.

"No, no, nothing at all. I want to get things straightened away before the baby comes." Eliza closed the box and pushed it back under the sofa. She climbed to her feet and dropped heavily into a wooden armchair. She rested her hands lightly on the bulge at the front of her dress.

"Can I get you something?" Charlotte asked. "Tea maybe?"

"Tea would be perfect," Eliza answered and Charlotte went into the kitchen to put on the kettle.

"How was school today?" Eliza asked when Charlotte came back.

"Good, good. The children need to do some catching up, but things seem fine. Eileen, Miss

McArthur, I mean, she left all her books and lesson plans. I can just start up again where she left off."

"She left stuff in the classroom?"

"Yes, I should really box it all up and send it to her. Do you have an address?"

"No, not at all. Best to ask my husband."

"Miss McArthur was planning a pageant for Thanksgiving. The children are very excited about it."

"We have one every year," Eliza said. "Pastor Miles will probably come by to talk to you about it. After the play, he usually gives a short sermon and leads a prayer."

Charlotte went to the kitchen, and returned balancing a cup and saucer in each hand. They sat quietly for a moment, drinking their tea. Charlotte felt Eliza studying her. Did Eliza think Charlotte was too young to be a teacher?

"I hope you are happy living here," Eliza said at last. "We don't provide very much in the line of entertainment."

So that was it. "This is my first school," Charlotte said. "I'll probably spend a lot of time to prepare for the classes. The Thanksgiving Pageant will take a lot of work."

"It will be a good chance for you to meet all the parents."

"I hope everyone will like it," Charlotte said.

Eliza nodded. "I hope I'll be able to come." And then she added, "Mrs. Ernest Miles called by today.

She's arranged a party for you tomorrow evening. She wants to introduce you to some of the other young ladies here in Bandit Creek."

"That's very thoughtful of her."

"Bandit Creek is a friendly place but the last few teachers have moved on. It's been hard on the children. I hope you'll be happy here."

· · · · ·

At Pastor Miles's home, the following evening, Charlotte had no problem believing Mrs. Miles was the minister's wife. Mabel Miles was a small woman, with bright blue eyes. Her hair pulled back from her face in a tight roll. She wore round eyeglasses that had no rims, only a gold bridge over her nose. She wore a black dress with a deep blue collar.

Charlotte realized that Mabel Miles had planned something far different from a party for her. It was more like an inquisition. There were other young women there, but Mrs. Miles spent half the evening finding out Charlotte's entire life history. That she had grown up on a farm near St. Helen in Michigan. That her parents and the rest of her family now lived in California. That she stayed in Michigan when her family moved because she loved school and wanted to be a teacher. That she had lived with her best friend, Ora Sharp, and her family while she went to Normal School. That this was her first teaching position.

Mabel was impressed by the grade eleven medal Charlotte had earned for being at the top of her class.

"Well, you may have finished Normal School, but do you have any experience taking care of children?" Mrs. Miles asked.

"I have six younger brothers and sisters. Five of us were born in five years. Mom had Jenny a few years later, and then Ben, who was the baby. You could say I have a lot of experience with kids."

Eventually, the pastor's wife patted her hand and said, "I think you'll do fine as the teacher. Now, if you need anything, you just let me know. My husband is one of the school trustees and I like to help him out."

Charlotte had a chance to meet the other girls when the older women gathered in the kitchen to help Mrs. Miles serve the coffee and cake.

"Sorry you had to go through all that," one of the girls, Ruth Kohler, whispered. "Mrs. Miles thinks she runs this town."

"I imagine she wanted to see if I was up to teaching in the school."

"We were lucky to get you to come so fast when Miss McArthur left all unexpected. My brothers and sisters were home and underfoot for three weeks."

"This was the first job offer I got," Charlotte confided. "My friend, Ora, was getting married, so… It was time for me to find a job." Charlotte changed the subject. "Do folks around here play cards?" she asked.

Ruth giggled. "Not at Mrs. Miles's place. Here we just drink tea and work on knitting or some such thing. But there's a dance at the Atherton Pavilion on Friday night."

"A dance would be wonderful but I don't know how I would get there."

"Would you like to come with us? I'll ask my mother if we can take you."

"A dance." Charlotte smiled and her feet began to tap in time to some imaginary music. "I wouldn't miss it for the world."

Chapter Ten

Friday morning Charlotte packed a bag with a change of clothes, a little hand-held mirror and her curling tongs. In her purse, she added some hairpins, a brush, and the Ladysmith Revolver.

When the rest of the family moved, her mother had been able to give Charlotte just a few things—Charlotte's blue trunk, the curling tongs and the Ladysmith. Her father bought the gun before he left for California. He taught both Charlotte and her mother how to shoot it.

Charlotte sighted the gun towards the floor and slid her finger against the trigger. The Ladysmith was the perfect size for her hand and could be hidden in her purse. It was unusual because it held seven bullets. She hadn't shot the gun since they left the farm. The revolver gave her a funny homesick feeling and she put it back in her purse.

Charlotte left the bag in the teacherage so she could change after school. It was a single room with a bed behind a screen in one corner, a table and some chairs and even a wooden rocking chair beside the woodstove. A coal oil lamp sat on the table. Charlotte could use it to heat up her curling tongs. She marveled at all the space. She'd never had a single room to herself.

At the Dredger place, she shared a room with the two girls, Maud and Elyse. Tommy was the youngest child, the only boy, and he had his own room. Charlotte envied him.

She crossed the breezeway to the schoolroom. Most of the children were already playing in the schoolyard. She would just have time to start a fire in the stove before it was time to ring the bell.

Seeing the classroom was still a heady experience for her. She still couldn't believe her luck in getting a teaching job. With a start, she realized she was not alone. There sitting at her desk was Luc Branigan. He had lit the fire and the room was already warm.

Calm down, she told herself. "Are you here to study grade four, Mr. Branigan? In grade four, we do long division."

"Very funny, Miss Fraser. No, I'm here to offer you a ride back to Dredger's ranch anytime you need one. In the winter, we always send someone for my brothers and sisters. We can drop you off at Dredger's road." Then, he smiled a charming smile. "And because I would like to invite you to a dance this evening."

"Oh, for the ride, thank you. As for the dance, no, I can't go with you."

"No? I thought you liked to dance?"

"Yes, I do. But I am going to the Atherton Pavilion with Ruth Kohler and her mother tonight."

It was too bad she couldn't go with the handsome cowboy.

"The Atherton Pavilion?" he repeated.

"Yes. Are there other places to dance around here?"

"For folks like you, the Pavilion is the main place. You can dance in the saloons, but I don't recommend it."

. . . . .

Riding in the stagecoach to the Atherton Pavilion was a first for Charlotte. She was lucky enough to sit beside the window of the coach, crowded in with Ruth, her mother and three other girls. They all wore their best dresses and filled the stagecoach with a flurry of colors. The wind blew in some gray clouds and the snow was falling lightly. She watched the flakes settle silently on the ground.

The Atherton Pavilion was a long white building set on the bank of the river. Unlike the homes in Bandit Creek, the Pavilion had electricity and it glowed in the night. Two electric pendant lights on either side of the front door lit up the pathway and the lights from the windows gleamed in the night. Inside, Japanese lanterns shimmered in the ballroom.

Charlotte looked around the hall. Things were so different here from back in St. Helen. A single fiddler, a tall dark-haired man wearing a buckskin jacket, provided the music. He played square dances, but the popular music was a new dance, the two-step, and as soon as he started the first one, dancers crowded onto the floor. Everyone was high-spirited. While some of the dancers were graceful, a lot were just exuberant.

Alec Forrest, the sheriff, stood alone at the back of the hall, watching her. She noticed how good-looking he was. She started to go over and thank him for helping her out on her first day in town.

Then Luc Branigan appeared at her side and asked her to dance. He guided Charlotte expertly around the dance floor, pulling her close to him when a miner brushed against them.

"Just a cowboy, Luc? You don't dance?" she asked, teasing him.

He gave her an "aw shucks" smile. "When women see what a great dancer I am, they can't keep away from me."

Soon, it was time to eat. Luc offered Charlotte his arm to guide her into the dining room. But the sheriff had come over from the back of the hall. "I'd like to escort the teacher for supper," he said.

Luc Branigan looked surprised. "Sheriff, I never expected to see you here." He turned to Charlotte and shrugged his shoulders as if to say what can I do? "Charlotte, this is the sheriff, Alec Forrest. He'll probably warn you all about me. Don't believe a word he says."

"Are you going to warn me about Luc Branigan?" she asked. "Otto Dredger already has."

"I want a word with you, Miss Fraser. And to enjoy your company at dinner." He offered his arm to her. She looked at Luc, and he nodded his consent.

"I got caught up in my office the other day. My deputy had arrested one of . . . a young lady. I needed to deal with that. When I came out, I saw you getting into the wagon with Luc, so I knew you would be fine."

The sheriff was explaining himself to Charlotte. She wondered if he was making an apology of sorts.

The tables in the dining room were set with china and big glass goblets. Fall vegetables, pumpkins, wheat sheaves and bright yellow napkins added color. Dinner was turkey and all of the trimmings. Charlotte tucked into her meal.

Sheriff Forrest watched Charlotte inhale the food. "Don't they feed you at the Dredger's place?"

Truth was, Eliza Dredger was too tired these days to cook very much and she didn't have any help in the house. Dinner was often what Charlotte put together after she got home from school. Not that she was going to complain about all that to Alec Forrest.

"You've hardly touched your dinner, Sheriff."

He ate his dinner slowly. "I don't often get a home cooked meal. I like to enjoy the experience."

Once they had finished eating, he said "Let's step outside for a bit."

"I don't think so." What kind of girl did he think she was?

"Don't worry. You're too young for me to be trifling with."

She laughed. "Okay, sheriff. I can't believe you're more than twenty or twenty-one. Just how old are you?"

He smiled. "I had to grow up fast."

Charlotte knew what that felt like. "Well, it's good to know I am safe with you."

"The point is that you're not safe here. I need to talk to you about Miss McArthur."

He took her out to a bandstand that sat at the back of the pavilion, on the edge of Bandit Creek. The creek ran silently with hardly a ripple, the moonlight playing over its black expanse. Charlotte shivered in her party dress.

"What do you know about Miss McArthur, Charlotte?"

"When I took this job, the letter from the school board said that she had left unexpectedly. All her things are still at the school, Sheriff. It puzzles me. I've only been a teacher for a few days but all of the lesson plans I made at Normal School, all of the posters I hang on the walls, I expect I'll take them with me when I go."

"And hers are all in the classroom," he commented. "I searched her desk to see if there was any sign of where she went. There wasn't anything."

"Her trunk is still at the Dredger's. She hasn't sent for it," Charlotte continued.

The sheriff, if possible, looked even more

concerned. "Charlotte, we can't keep a teacher in this town. Most of them move after a few months. Only one of them stayed to marry someone and that was Otto Dredger's wife. And now Miss McArthur has disappeared like this."

"So do you think something happened to her?" Charlotte asked.

"That's what I'm trying to find out."

Charlotte shivered. If it could happen to one teacher, it could happen to her. Alone, without any family in this remote mining town. "Do you think I'm going to be next?"

"My job is to not let it come to that. I want you to keep your eyes open. And let me know if anything seems unusual to you. Anything that strikes you as wrong. Do you know what I mean?"

"Play detective?"

"No, don't play detective. Come to me the minute you feel anything is wrong."

He touched her cheek gently. "Be careful, Charlotte Fraser. Something here is not right."

He strode away, around the building towards the road.

Charlotte watched him go. She could still feel his touch on her cheek.

For the first time in days, she was all alone. She looked around to see if anyone was coming out, but no, she had the bandstand to herself. Charlotte watched Bandit Creek flow past. The snow had stopped falling and the clouds were gone. The sky was clear and stars twinkled down on her.

Behind her, she heard the door on the pavilion close. She turned around to see Luc Branigan crossing the grounds towards her.

"I wondered where you got to," he said.

She watched him approach.

"I saw you come out here with the sheriff. Where did he go?"

"Off doing sheriff work, I imagine. He seems like a man with a mission."

"Only here four days, and the sheriff wants to talk to you. What have you been up to?"

"He wanted to ask me about Eileen McArthur. It's so strange how she just disappeared like that."

He was silent for a minute. "People around here have been talking about it. Wondering if she went off with one of the miners or went back to Texas where she came from."

"Did you know her very well?"

"Who me? No. I don't think she had time for a simple cowboy." There was an edge in his voice.

"I think you're a whole lot more than a simple cowboy."

"Do you?" He sounded pleased. He took one of her blond ringlets and twisted it around a finger. He tugged on it gently. When she didn't resist, he slid his hand over her cheek and under her chin. Charlotte gazed into Luc Branigan's eyes and for a moment felt lost in them.

Luc slid his free arm around her and pulled her

towards him. Taking his time, he kissed her.

She pulled away gently. "I've only been here four days," she said, repeating his words back to him. "We should go inside."

"Indeed." He smiled. He slid his arm down her back and let it rest for a moment at her waist. He guided her back towards the pavilion. She liked the possessive way his arm felt on her back.

Chapter Eleven

Back at the ranch, Charlotte closed the door quietly behind herself. She wondered if she could get into bed without waking up the girls, Maud and Elyse.

As she crossed the floor to the staircase, the door to Otto Dredger's den flew open.

She gave a little gasp. "Oh, it's you, Mr. Dredger."

He stood in the doorway. "I've startled you, I see."

"I thought everyone was in bed." She kept her voice low.

"Come in here and tell me about your evening," he said, retreating into the den.

Charlotte was happy, but bone-tired. "The dance went on until midnight, and then we took the stagecoach back to Bandit Creek." She followed him. "It must be really late."

"Close the door. We don't want to wake up everyone."

She closed the door and sank into a chair. He had a bottle of whiskey open and two glasses. Without asking, he poured her a shot and passed it over.

Was he waiting up for her?

"What time is it?" She took a small sip of the

whiskey. It burned her throat.

Mr. Dredger took out a gold pocket watch and opened the case. "It's just going on two. You'll have a hard time in the morning when the children all get up. Hard to keep them quiet."

He played with the watch, opening it and closing it. "It's a beautiful watch," Charlotte said.

"Yes," he said, handing it to her. "It was my grandfather's. He gave it to me back in Texas."

She traced her finger over the shape of a thistle carved into the case. "Was he Scottish?"

"No, why would you think that?"

"Scotland's emblem is the thistle."

"Well, he wasn't Scottish. He was German. And this is my sister, Laura," he said, opening the watch and looking at a picture of a girl. "She was pretty and smart. She was a schoolteacher, just like you."

"You must miss her," Charlotte said, thinking for a minute about all her younger brothers and sisters. "Did something happen to her?"

"No, no." He snapped the watch closed before Charlotte could see the picture more closely. "Nothing happened to her. She's still back in Texas." He had a faraway look in his eyes, as if he too was back in Texas with his sister.

He put the watch back into his pocket. "Tell me about the dance tonight."

"It was wonderful. Have you been to the Atherton Pavilion?"

He nodded.

"Well, then you know what it's like. There was a turkey dinner and then we danced until midnight. Everyone was friendly and I danced almost every dance."

"Was Luc Branigan there?"

"Yes," she said, slowly. "So many people have warned me about him."

"Who?

"You for one, Sheriff Forrest, for another." That wasn't strictly true. Luc had said the sheriff would warn her about himself, but they hadn't talked about him at all. "Why do you ask?"

"You're a beautiful girl, Charlotte. Pretty and smart like my sister. A lot of men would want you for their own."

She sipped her whiskey.

He reached over and stroked her arm. "A lot of men would want you," he repeated.

Suddenly she felt very much alone, in a house filled with people. "It's late," she said. "I should get to bed."

He put out the lights and followed her up the staircase. He caught her arm as she was about to open the door to her bedroom. "Sleep well, sweet Charlotte." Before she could stop him, he dropped a kiss on her forehead. It was almost as if he was kissing his daughter goodnight.

Almost.

Chapter Twelve

The next morning over breakfast, Charlotte made plans to go into town to work on the Thanksgiving Pageant. She already had some marking to do. Otto Dredger told Charlotte she could ride Eliza's horse into town, if she liked. Charlotte looked over at Eliza, who merely smiled and said it would be good for the horse to have someone riding her.

Down in the barn, Charlotte found Lee and asked him to help her saddle up the mare. He took a sidesaddle down from a bar.

"I don't ride sidesaddle," Charlotte told him.

"You ride like a man?" he asked, incredulous. "I don't know what Mr. Dredger would say about that."

"Well, my mother and father let me ride astride and that's what I'm going to do."

"Okay," he said, shaking his head. "Don't say I didn't warn you."

She was out of the barn and down the road before anyone else could express an opinion about how a lady ought to ride a horse. Really, this was 1911. Only last year, Two-Gun Nan Aspinwall had ridden astride all of the way from San Francisco to New York. If anyone objected to her split skirts when she rode through their town, she shot up the place until everyone left her alone.

Charlotte thought for a moment about the little gun in her purse. She couldn't imagine shooting up Bandit Creek if anyone gave her any trouble about riding like a man. No proper teacher would do that.

· · · · ·

Sheriff Forrest slowly paged through the papers on the teacher's desk in the schoolroom for the second time. He noticed that the new teacher had taken all of Miss McArthur's things and put them into the bottom drawer. There was nothing new to find. Charlotte's notes and lesson plans covered the desk. He got up to leave and Charlotte rode by the window on her horse.

"Well, if that doesn't beat all," he said. The girl was riding her horse like a man. The young women in this town gave him no end of trouble and it looked like Charlotte would be no exception.

He went outside and watched her slide off the horse. She turned around to tie the horse to a rail, and Alec could see the outline of her bottom through the back of her pants.

"What in hell are you doing in those pants?" he yelled at her.

"It's a skirt," she said, turning around to show him the front of it. He had to admit she looked cute in her riding outfit, but that wasn't the point.

"What are you doing in my schoolroom?" she asked.

"Listen to me, Charlotte. You can't go around here riding your horse like a man. It's not seemly. Before you know it, Mrs. Miles will be insisting that I arrest you. And what are you wearing?" He waved at her skirt. She had sewn a split in the back that let her ride astride.

"In a town where there are prostitutes living over the bar, why would anyone care how I ride a horse?"

"Because, Charlotte, you are the teacher. You're not one of those dance hall girls, although you give me about as much trouble as some of them do."

She was silent for a minute. It looked like she was trying to decide if she should keep arguing with him or not. "It's not right. To even mount a horse sidesaddle, you always need someone to help you."

"It may not be right, Charlotte, but you have to decide if you want to live in this town or not," he said as gently as he could manage.

"How do you expect me to get back home if I can't ride this horse?" she demanded.

He sighed. "After you're finished up here at the school, come by my house." He pointed out a house down the road from the school. "At least, let me ride back to the ranch with you. Nobody will make a fuss if I'm with you."

. . . . .

Charlotte spent the day working on the Thanksgiving Pageant. Every student, even the little ones, needed to have at least one line to say.

The script was the place to start. She took a history book from the book shelf and turned to the first Thanksgiving. She needed characters to be Indian princesses and native men. She needed Pilgrim Fathers and Pilgrim women and children. Charlotte made a list and started on the script.

She drew some hats for the Pilgrim Fathers on brown paper. The children could cut them out and color them. She made another list of things to do and things to make, paper dresses for the Indian princesses and headbands for some of the boys.

Charlotte drew a picture of a turkey. She had the idea that some of the smaller children could pin drawings of pumpkins and turkeys to their clothes to dress up as the first Thanksgiving meal.

She pondered over what to use for the Mayflower. She was excited about the whole project and could hardly wait for Monday morning when the children would start working on it.

· · · · ·

Charlotte was about to knock on the sheriff's door, when he came out of the house following a man wearing a black wool vest over a white shirt and a black tie. Despite the weather, the man wasn't wearing a jacket.

"There's trouble over at the Golden Nugget," Alec said. "Go in and make yourself at home. I won't be gone long."

She was intrigued by the opportunity to check out his house. It was a bungalow, with two built-in bookcases separating the living room from the dining room. There was a stone fireplace in the living room but no fire in the grate. Beside it, in a corner stood an upright piano. At the back of the house was a little galley kitchen. There was a fire burning in the wood stove which made it the coziest room in the house.

The bookcases were filled with classics. Imagine that, an educated sheriff. The piano was a surprise. She leafed through some of the music in the piano bench and found one of her favorites, the Merry Oldsmobile song.

Charlotte played a few bars and then repeated them. She worked her way through the song line by line, until she could play it smoothly. The next time through, when she got to the chorus, she began to sing.

"Come away with me, Lucille, in my merry Oldsmobile." Charlotte heard a noise and turned around to see the sheriff watching her.

"That was my mother's favorite song," he said. "My parents had an Oldsmobile." He took a picture from the mantle above the fireplace and handed it to her. In the picture, a man, a woman, and a boy stood beside a car.

"It's my mom and dad," he said. "And me. On our way out west."

"Fancy car," she said.

He smiled briefly. "I still have it. That Oldsmobile was my dad's pride and joy." Then his smile disappeared. "Probably the reason they were shot."

"What?" Charlotte was shocked. He sounded so matter of fact.

"They were shot in a hold-up. The bandits let me go. The sheriff here in Bandit Creek, Dan Wilson, took me and made me a deputy. He let me help him hunt those bandits down.

"I was small for my age. If I'd been any bigger, they probably would have shot me, too."

Charlotte let out a little breath. She softly played a chord. "It must have been really tough. Hunting down the men who killed your parents."

"It took us about a year to get all three of them. We shipped them off to Missoula for trial. I had to testify." He still sounded so unsentimental. Charlotte realized he didn't want to show emotion. She wished there was something she could do for him.

"If it was me, I would hate to stay here and be reminded of what happened to your parents."

"The sheriff made me go to school. The town folk were like a family to me. Bandit Creek became my home."

He seemed strong, and lonely . . . she knew exactly how he felt. She wanted to go over to him and stroke his brow. Instead, she played a few more bars of the song. "Do you want me to stop?"

"No," he said. "I like it."

Chapter Thirteen

Sunday morning, Charlotte rode Eliza Dredger's horse to church and back. Sidesaddle. Otto had insisted because, apparently, it was necessary if she was going to be the teacher in Bandit Creek. Her spirits were low.

Otto Dredger was riding, too, but he wanted Charlotte to go on ahead. She passed the wagon carrying Eliza Dredger and the girls. She wondered where Tommy was.

It was the first time she had ever ridden sidesaddle, despite it being the only proper way for a lady to ride. She had more control of the horse than she expected, but she needed to use the whip instead of leg commands on both sides. At first, she felt unsteady, and it took a while to find the right combination of balance and posture to feel secure.

With the wind in her hair, she relaxed for a moment and enjoyed the sunshine and the sound of melting water. The snow was beginning to recede. The roads were turning into a bumpy washboard.

Charlotte had a moment's thought for Eliza Dredger who was riding over those bumps in the carriage. If that didn't bring the baby on, Charlotte didn't know what would. She felt bad for the woman. Mrs. Dredger clearly didn't want to make the trip to town this morning, but Mr. Dredger had insisted. He reminded her that she wouldn't have many chances to get out after the baby came. Eliza had resisted but, in the end, her husband's concern for her happiness overrode her hesitation.

Charlotte got to the church early to meet the Reverend Miles. He was going to lead the prayers at the Thanksgiving Pageant at the school. He told her that it had become a tradition in Bandit Creek, and it was always in the morning so that everyone could go home and be with their families for the day.

She didn't know what to do about the Mayflower, but Reverend Miles told her he had built and painted a replica a few years earlier. They stored it in the church basement and the older boys would know where to find it.

Charlotte smiled. "You built it yourself?"

"Ministers can be just as handy as anyone else."

. . . . .

Charlotte was the first one back from church. Lee, one of the ranch hands, led her horse over to a fence so she could climb down. It was still cold, and the horse was covered with sweat. Charlotte told Lee she would take care of it, and she led the horse around the corner to the barn.

Ahead of her, she could see the unmistakable figure of Annie Hamilton crossing the yard into the barn, young Tommy hanging on to one hand.

Charlotte followed them into the barn. Annie was kneeling on the dirt floor comforting the boy.

"Mommy, I want to come with you," Tommy said.

"Remember, this is our secret," Annie said to the boy.

"I can keep secrets."

Charlotte was horrified. "You're his mother?" she asked. "Tommy is too young to keep that a secret. It's not fair on the boy."

Annie frowned at Charlotte. She turned back to the boy. "Go back into the house now and wait for your father." Annie gave him a deep hug and whispered something in his ear. Tommy turned and walked slowly out the barn door.

Charlotte pulled the horse closer to her. "The boy must be confused."

"He can keep this a secret. He has to."

"It's not fair to him." Charlotte was upset.

"You need to keep this to yourself."

Charlotte just looked at her.

"Don't you be looking at me like that," Annie said. "It's for Tommy's sake. If folks around here knew I was his mother, life would be really hard for him."

"He's six years old. How has he kept the secret this long?"

"I only told him a few months ago. Before that, he thought I was his aunt."

Charlotte bit her lip. She had nothing to say.

Annie grasped Charlotte's arms. "Will you keep this to yourself? Folks around here think Eliza is his mother. It's not for me. It's for Tommy."

Charlotte nodded. "Tommy is a great kid. But you must know he won't be able to keep silent forever."

"I'm taking him away soon, so I had to tell him."

"Do the Dredgers know that?"

"I've paid Otto Dredger for Tommy's room and board since I left him here. He knows I want to take Tommy away."

"What about Eliza?" Charlotte asked.

"It would be better for her if I take him. It's hard on her, the lying, pretending that Tommy is her son. She has two kids of her own. And another on the way."

"And Mr. Dredger is his father?"

"That much is true," Annie said. She took her horse out of a stall and led it to the barn door.

"Wait," Charlotte said. "There's something I need to ask you."

"What?"

Charlotte took off her hat and inclined her head towards Annie. Dark roots were growing in behind her blond curls.

"Well, well," Annie laughed. "The new schoolteacher dyes her hair. Folks around here will be shocked."

"Back in Kalamazoo, my friend, Ora, and I went to a beauty parlor and had our hair dyed. We did it on a dare. I like it but if it grows any longer, everyone will be able to see that I dyed it. And here I am, in the middle of nowhere, with no place to buy any more hair dye."

"I do know what people will think," Annie said.

"Can you help me out? I went past the store the other day, but the only kind of cosmetics they have is Pond's Cold Cream."

"I can get you some hair dye. Come by my place, Tuesday after school. From the front, it's the Men's Club beside the Powder Horn Saloon. Walk down the lane and come up the back way. There's a stairway there. No one will see you."

"Where do you get it from?"

"They sell it at the store, but they keep it under the counter. I'll get some for you tomorrow."

Charlotte followed Annie out of the barn. Annie rode her horse astride, no sidesaddle for her. She took the road leading up towards the mine. It was farther to get to town that way, but she would be able to cross Bandit Creek at the ford and circle back to the stables without anyone seeing her.

Tommy was playing in the yard. "Come on inside with me," Charlotte said. "We'll start lunch for your mother."

Tommy looked relieved. "You can keep a secret," he said. "That's good, or I'd be in trouble with my dad."

Chapter Fourteen

Tuesday, after school, Charlotte climbed up the backstairs of the building where Annie Hamilton lived above the Men's Club. Most of the other girls were gone already, to the Powder Horn Saloon next door. Annie was dressed in a simple white dress with an apron over it. She looked like any wife, dressed to do her housework.

The hair dye process was a two-step procedure. First Annie applied some bleach along the roots of Charlotte's hair and let it sit for a while. She rinsed it out and applied a concoction that looked like bits of flowers and some chalk. It was a pasty mess that would give her hair a golden yellow color.

"I really appreciate you doing this for me."

"It's nothing," Annie said. "This is a chance for me to find out how Tommy's doing in school."

"He's just in Grade One but he already knows how to read. He follows along when I'm teaching Grade Two. He's a clever boy and he's not always falling off his bench like some of the other little boys."

Annie was silent for a minute, thinking about her son. "Thank you Charlotte. Most of the teachers would never talk to me. But then, none of them knew that I'm his mother."

"Did you ever meet Eileen McArthur?"

"She would cross the street when she saw me coming," Annie said. "The last time I saw her was the night she disappeared. It was practically dark and she was walking home alone."

"It's all so strange," Charlotte said. "She left her stuff at the school and her trunk is still in my bedroom at the Dredger place. It's almost like she's coming back."

"In that little room? Do you still have to share with Maud?"

"And Elyse, too. How did you know that?" Charlotte asked.

"I used to be the teacher here."

"Oh." A bastard son fathered by a married man would end any teaching career.

"Have you ever had your hair waved?" Annie asked.

"No, can you do that, too?"

"Sure." Annie heated a plate and applied it to Charlotte's hair. Charlotte looked in the mirror and saw blond waves. "Hey, I look like I'm eighteen." Delighted, she said, "Annie, you could open one of those beauty parlors. You know, like Elizabeth Arden in New York. I went to one, back in Kalamazoo."

"Not in this town, I couldn't," Annie said. "None of the women would ever come to me."

· · · · ·

Charlotte ran down the backstairs of Annie's place straight into the sheriff.

"What the hell are you doing in a brothel?" he demanded. This girl was going to be trouble.

"Men's Club," she said. "It's a Men's Club."

"Charlotte." He let go of an exasperated sigh. "What were you doing up there?"

"I was visiting Annie. She used to be the schoolteacher here. I wanted to see if she had any idea what happened to Eileen McArthur."

"And did she?"

"No, she didn't. I have to run, Sheriff. It's getting late and Luc Branigan is going to drop me off on his way home." She turned and hurried away.

He watched her disappear down the alley. Charlotte looked angelic with her blond hair, but there was something different about it. She looked a little more stylish today.

He hadn't thought of talking to Annie Hamilton about the missing schoolteacher. Charlotte was a smart girl but he never intended that she should go around talking to people about Eileen McArthur. He would have to talk to her again, and tell her to keep out of this mess.

But he had to admit that Charlotte was quite a girl. Filled with enthusiasm about her job, and in many ways fearless. Cute as a button and she could play the piano, too. Listening to her play had brought back memories of his parents. It had never occurred to him that he might have a family again.

His job as sheriff here in Bandit Creek could be dangerous, and there was no room for a woman.

A lot of the sheriff's work in Bandit Creek consisted of keeping a lid on the brothels and breaking up fights in the saloons. There were four brothels in town, but the Men's Club located right on Main Street was a high-class establishment. They had their share of miners who were employed in the local gold and copper mine, but many of the clients were wealthy men from around the town. They could simply disappear into the laneway and arrive at Annie's place by the back steps.

Things could heat up when a miner fell in love with one of the girls, but the girls all had contracts with the owner of the brothel where they worked. The owners weren't about to stand by and see one of their girls run away, still owing money. Some poor miner often ended up getting shot.

Alec knew his way around the rooms over the Men's Club. Like most men, he preferred to use the back stairs.

He found Annie down in her room. She was clearing away something that had the harsh smell of bleach.

"Miss Hamilton? How are you?" he asked politely.

Annie laughed. "You're the only person who calls me that anymore."

"Old habits die hard. And you were my favorite teacher."

"What can I do for you, Sheriff?"

"Tell me what you know about Eileen McArthur."

"There's nothing to tell, Sheriff. I never met her, and we never spoke."

Her offhand manner was a dead giveaway. "Is there something you're not telling me, Miss Hamilton?"

. . . . .

After the sheriff left, Annie took her time getting ready for her first Tuesday evening visitor. As she changed clothes, she thought about her conversation with Luc Branigan the day Eileen McArthur had disappeared.

Luc had been drinking and he'd stopped her on the street outside the Powder Horn. He was angry and kept asking her if she thought Dredger was taking an interest in Miss McArthur. Luc knew Otto Dredger had been Annie's lover, and maybe Otto had been boasting about his way with women again.

They saw Miss McArthur cross the street to avoid them, and Luc got even angrier, if that was possible. That's when he had left her. As she watched him walk away, she saw Tommy a block ahead, carrying a lantern. Luc's conduct was strange, and why would Tommy be in town? But what could she say to the sheriff about this?

She thought about coming to teach in Bandit Creek. Luc was a young cowboy working on his father's ranch. She used to see him every day when he picked up his brothers and sisters at school. He would often drive her back to the Dredger ranch where she was boarding. She had imagined she was in love with the handsome cowboy, but then Otto Dredger turned his charm on her. She'd been so foolish. And with a married man. What had she been thinking? When Luc found out he had been so angry, and so hurt.

On that day a month ago in October, was Luc angry about losing another woman to Dredger?

· · · · ·

Annie poured the sherry when she recognized Pastor Miles's step on the stairs.

The pastor was excited this evening and couldn't wait to tell her his good news. He had been offered a new church in Seattle. It was in a city and had a bigger congregation.

The time passed quickly and it was nearly time for him to leave before he led her to the bed. Tonight he wanted to sit and watch her undress.

Annie had sex with many men, but few of them were concerned about her pleasure. The pastor was the exception. He knew how to touch her, where to stroke, how to excite her. It seemed to increase his pleasure to be able to arouse her, and truth be told, with him, the act was not as much of a chore as it was with her other clients. Sometimes she wondered how he had learned to be so skillful.

When they were finished, he lay beside her for a few minutes, holding her.

"I'll be sad to see you leave," Annie said. "You, of all my guests."

"Would you say that to anyone?" he asked, his voice suddenly serious.

"Most men don't really care what I feel," she said. "There's no need for me to say anything."

"You could come with me," he said slowly.

"You and me and Mrs. Miles? Somehow, I don't think that will work."

He turned her head to face him. "You don't understand. It's a new life for me, a new start. You can be part of my new life. I want you to come with me. We'll introduce you as my wife. No one needs to know about all of this."

"Me, the minister's wife. I can't imagine it."

"Annie, I knew you when you were the teacher here. You will do just fine."

"What about your wife? You can't just leave her here."

"Honestly, Annie, she doesn't want to come. Things have changed between us so much. She loves our house and she loves living in Bandit Creek. She would still have all that."

"How do you know she doesn't want to go with you?"

"She wants me to go ahead without her. Find a new house. Then she wants me to send for her. I know she won't come. I'm leaving after Thanksgiving. If she wanted to come with me, she'd come then."

Annie looked at the ceiling. She honestly didn't believe that Pastor Miles was the kind of man who would abandon his wife.

"What if she changes her mind?" she said. "I have a son. I've been saving my money to leave Bandit Creek and take him with me. I thought I might open a little business, like a hat maker or a dressmaker. Now I'm thinking—maybe a beauty salon."

"I always wanted a son," he said.

"Me, the minister's wife," she said again. This time she was smiling.

· · · · ·

Dredger came for his money that night. "Any news?" he asked. "Have you heard anything about the Ellis Mine?"

"One of the miners was complaining he had to work Thanksgiving Day when the mine is supposed to be closed. They're loading up a shipment to bring into town for the four o'clock train. He said they have to stay at the mine until two o'clock and he wants to be at home with his family."

Dredger took a sip of his whiskey and saluted her with his glass. "I always like it when someone pays a debt they owe me."

Annie took the hint and gave him the last of the money she owed him. Otto had insisted she pay for her room and board and for the doctor when Tommy was born. It had taken her a long time to save the money.

"After this, I won't owe you anything

"But you need to keep paying me for the boy's room and board."

"It's not fair that I have to pay you for Tommy."

"He's your son, Annie."

"He's your son, too."

"Is he? Sometimes I wonder if there wasn't someone else."

"Otto, you know that's not true." Annie took a deep breath. "I'm leaving Bandit Creek. On Thanksgiving. I want to take Tommy with me."

He had always said she was welcome to take the boy as soon as she paid him back the money she owed him.

He just shrugged. "Fine, take him with you."

Chapter Fifteen

In the morning, Charlotte assigned the roles in the Thanksgiving Pageant. All of the girls wanted to be Indian princesses, but Charlotte needed some of them to be Pilgrims as well.

One little girl, Nellie Welch, came up to Charlotte's desk and explained that she had to be an Indian princess because her mother had made her a special Indian princess dress. That was when Charlotte realized the pageant had taken on a life of its own.

Eventually, Charlotte got all of the roles sorted out and the children started learning their lines. Dylan Branigan was being his usual energetic self, so Charlotte took him to one side and explained that she had a very special job for him. He had to learn everybody's lines in case anyone missed the pageant. The show must go on and it would be up to him to fill in. It was a huge job, but Dylan promised Charlotte he could do it.

Tommy Dredger wanted to be the Indian, Squanto, so Charlotte got him busy making a headdress. Somewhere, he found some feathers. After seeing Tommy's headdress, all of the boys wanted to be Indians, but Charlotte convinced some of them that they had to be Pilgrims.

The very little children would be turkeys, a deer,

some corn and a pumpkin. They had just a few words each to say and Charlotte had them rehearse their lines together.

The next week passed quickly as Charlotte adjusted to her new life in Bandit Creek. When it got colder, Luc Branigan or one of the men from the Branigan ranch was always ready to pick up the Branigan children at school. Charlotte and the Dredger kids would catch a ride as far as the turnoff to the Dredger ranch.

Despite the friction between the families, it was pretty clear that Tommy Dredger and Dylan Branigan were best friends. They were two years apart in age and always played together in the schoolyard.

One day after school, Charlotte was walking on the bridge over the creek and she saw Luc Branigan and the two boys skipping rocks at the ford. Luc looked like a boy himself, as he sent the rocks skimming along

When they finished playing, Tommy crossed the creek to Dredger's land. Luc's voice carried through the crisp air. "Don't tell your dad you were out here playing with us, Tommy. It has to be our secret."

Poor Tommy, how many secrets was the boy expected to keep?

. . . . .

Saturday afternoon, Mr. Dredger offered to take Charlotte on a tour of the ranch. They went out to the barn and Lee saddled up the mare for her. She looked at the sidesaddle with resignation.

"Let me help you up on that horse," Otto Dredger offered.

His hands lingered for a second as he grasped her waist.

"I've a spot that I want to show you," he said, leading the way along the creek. After about a mile, he turned onto a path that climbed up the base of Crow Mountain.

"You need to follow me exactly," Mr. Dredger said. "There are a lot of shafts dug into this mountain from the gold rush days. You could easily fall into one."

He led the way to the top of a cliff. When he helped Charlotte dismount, he let her body slide along his.

"You're so lovely," he said. "I can't stop myself from thinking about what it would be like to touch you." His voice was kind. "But you can trust me to be a gentleman, Charlotte."

She looked at him. He must be almost as old as her father. Besides, he was a married man.

He turned and led her down a path from the cliff to a ledge below.

"I found this ledge when I was mining this property. There's a cave at the back of it where I worked a vein of gold. The gold is all gone now, but that's how I got my start in Montana."

Charlotte could see the steeple of the church in Bandit Creek, but the rest of the town was hidden behind the trees.

"This is my special place, Charlotte. We can see the whole valley, but no one can see us. I love to come here and wonder about the beauty of it all."

"It's breathtaking, Mr. Dredger."

"Call me Otto. I feel like we can be friends." Mr. Dredger pointed out the creek below. "My land is everything on this side of the creek. The other side is the Branigan ranch."

"The main road runs farther south, and that little trail along the creek goes out to the Ellis mine. It's a back road. They use it when they want to move things without a lot of attention. The Ellis brothers don't know I can see everything that goes by from this ledge."

He pointed to a waterfall. "That's Deadman's Falls. Branigan's father was found there five years ago. Probably some miner robbed him and dumped him in the creek. His body washed up at the foot of the falls."

Charlotte peered down into the gorge. She could see the waterfall below and the trail snaking around it. Part of the creek was frozen over, but the waterfall splashed onto the snow and ice and left a track of water down one side.

When Charlotte leaned farther out over the edge, Mr. Dredger pushed her a little and she grasped hold of him for safety. As he intended.

"Charlotte? Do you feel what I feel?" he whispered. He pulled her closer. "I've got you. You're safe with me." He tried to give her a kiss but she turned her face away.

Charlotte pushed herself away from him, away from the edge. Really, what was he thinking? She felt outraged, but she didn't know what to say to him, alone on the ledge. She turned and ran up the path to the top of the cliff.

"Let's ride down and see the waterfall," she said.

Mr. Dredger's playfulness was gone when he lifted her back onto the horse. Charlotte wished she didn't need his help. It felt creepy.

They were both quiet as they rode down the cliff. The sun was as warm as a spring day. They could hear the trickle of water dripping onto the trail.

Charlotte saw a navy blue patch in the melting snow. "Look at that," she said. She was stuck up on her horse and had no intention of letting Mr. Dredger help her down again. He dismounted and poked at the blue fabric with a stick. Charlotte rode closer. She could see the outline of a body, face down in the ice and snow. Some tufts of brown hair stuck out from the snow. Seeing the body was shock enough, but Charlotte felt her stomach heave when she saw that the arms of the body were bound with a cord.

"Oh my God," she cried.

"It looks like Eileen McArthur," Mr. Dredger

said. He pushed more of the snow away. "Go back and send out a couple of the boys. I'll need some help here."

"Okay. And then I'll go and get the sheriff." She rode away. She could hear him say something, but she just kept on riding.

Charlotte stopped in the ranch yard just long enough to tell the two ranch hands that Mr. Dredger needed them out by Deadman's Falls. Then she wheeled her horse around and took the road to Bandit Creek.

· · · · ·

Charlotte rode straight to the sheriff's office. She felt like an idiot stuck up on that horse and cursed the saddle. The deputy, Frank Waters, saw her through the window, and stepped outside.

"I need to see Alec—the sheriff."

A moment later, Alec Forrest emerged.

"Get me down off this stupid saddle." She could not keep the anger out of her voice. The sidesaddle was driving her crazy. He couldn't help but laugh. He helped her down, and steadied her with a hand on either shoulder.

"What's going on?" he asked.

"I was out riding with Otto Dredger. He was showing me the waterfall at Deadman's Gap. Miss McArthur was there. She's dead. She's been buried in the snow all this time. Her hands are tied. Mr. Dredger and a couple of the boys are bringing her body back to the ranch right now."

He didn't look like he was laughing now. "Can you ride back to the ranch with me?" he asked.

Charlotte thought of Mr. Dredger's hands sliding over her body. "I will never ride sidesaddle, ever again, even if it means I have to walk."

He sighed. "Okay, I'll get my car and drive you back."

Chapter Sixteen

At the Dredger ranch, Charlotte followed Alec into the house.

"I understand you've found a body," Alec said. Mr. Dredger nodded.

"I'll need to see it. And where you found it in the first place."

"Sheriff, I'm sorry Charlotte dragged you all of the way out here. There's been a drowning."

"I need to look at the body," Alec repeated.

"It's out in the barn. It'll stay colder there. I sent a couple of the boys out to make a box for her."

"You're arranging for the burial?"

"It's the least I can do. She lived with us and I feel responsible for her."

Alec nodded before he went out the door. Charlotte, still wearing her coat and boots, followed the two men. Out in the barn, Lee and Straws were hammering some lumber into a box.

"Where is she?" Mr. Dredger asked.

Lee pointed. "Still in the wagon, Boss. We had to put her on her face, because her hands were frozen behind her back. I had to chop her out of the ice."

Mr. Dredger held the light for Alec to see the body. Charlotte caught a glimpse of the white hands. She shuddered.

"It's been four weeks. I'm surprised the animals didn't get to her," Mr. Dredger said.

Alec tried to lift up one of her hands. "What do you think happened to her?"

"She probably walked too close to the river and fell in."

"You think she drowned?" Charlotte interrupted.

"Of course I do," Mr. Dredger replied. "What other explanation is there when she was in the water like that?"

"But her arms were tied together, bound with a rawhide cord."

Both men turned to look at Charlotte.

"You're saying she was murdered?" Alec asked.

"I saw a cord."

Alec turned to Lee. "Was there a cord on her hands?"

"Yeah, there was a leather strap. I cut it off so we could fit her in the box."

Alec picked up the piece of leather that lay beside the body. "Is this it?"

"Yes, sir, Sheriff Forrest."

Alec picked up the strap and looked at it. "You can find these on any ranch. Not much of a clue to who did this. Turn her over for me, would you?"

Neither man seemed like he wanted to touch the body, but they did so, turning her gently.

Charlotte gasped. The face was a frozen mask with the mouth open and the eyes closed.

Grotesque. The hair on the corpse was still frozen and, amazingly, was perfectly held back by two tortoise shell combs.

Mr. Dredger said, "Charlotte, you don't want to see this. Go back in the house."

Alec climbed up into the wagon. He knelt beside the body. "Hold that light closer."

He ripped open the coat, the ice crackling as he broke through the blue fabric. The woman's white shirt was red with the stain of blood near to her heart. Alec put his finger on the hole in her breast. "She didn't drown. She's been shot."

He tore away the blouse. "No doubt about it. Get me some pliers, boys, and a knife."

Lee found a pair on a workbench. Alec dug around with the knife, and then used the pliers to pull out a bullet.

"Oh, yeah, she's been shot all right." Alec climbed out of the wagon.

Mr. Dredger raised his light. "What's this?" he asked. Around the dead girl's neck was a chain threaded through a gold ring. He snapped the chain from around her neck. "Looks like a wedding ring."

"A wedding ring?" Alec looked at the ring and chain in Mr. Dredger's hand.

"I'm sure she wasn't married," Mr. Dredger said. "It's one of the things we find out before we hire a new teacher. Maybe it belonged to her mother. I'll put it with the rest of her things, in case her family comes to claim them."

Alec nodded. "That ring is the least of her worries now."

"We're through here." Mr. Dredger turned to Straws and Lee. "Put her in the box."

The two cowboys gingerly lifted the corpse.

"Close it up, boys," Alec directed, and they placed the pine lid onto the coffin. Charlotte's last view of Eileen McArthur, was a flash of brown hair frozen around the mask of her face.

She followed Alec and Mr. Dredger back into the house and into Mr. Dredger's den.

"Miss Fraser," Alec said. "You shouldn't have seen that."

"I felt like I had to, Sheriff. She could have been me. I could have been her. She was the teacher. I could be dead like that." Charlotte's hands began to shiver and her whole body began to shake. She was afraid she was going to cry.

"She needs something to steady her nerves." Mr. Dredger took his bottle of bourbon and three glasses from the cabinet. He filled two of them to the top. Then he filled one half full, and gave it to Charlotte.

"Here girl, drink this. It will stop the shaking."

"Are you going to be okay, Charlotte?" Alec reached over and chaffed her hands gently. "That was an awful sight."

Charlotte only nodded.

Mr. Dredger leaned back in his leather armchair. "If that doesn't beat all. The teacher shot on her way home from school."

Alec turned again to Charlotte. "How did you find the body?"

Charlotte felt drained. She collected her thoughts. "We were out riding," she began. "The sun was shining and the snow was starting to melt."

"Where did you see the body?"

"We were riding the track from the top of the cliff down to the river. I saw her near the waterfall . . ." She saw the body again in her mind. "At first, I could just see some blue fabric and I called out to Mr. Dredger. He got off his horse and poked at it with a stick. I rode closer and then I could see it was a person."

"Did you know who she was?"

"Looking at her clothes. They were blue." Charlotte pictured the sight, blue coat surrounded by snow and ice. "I thought it must be Miss McArthur."

"How would you know her clothes?" Alec asked.

"I saw a picture in my desk. It was a couple, a man and a woman. Someone had painted colors over the picture, you know, to make the skin look like flesh tones. Her dress, coat, and hat were all blue. When I saw the body, I knew it was her. I mean, who else could it be?

"Anyway," Charlotte continued, "I came back to the house and sent two of the cowboys out to help Mr. Dredger."

Alec turned to Mr. Dredger. "Of course, you

recognized the body."

"Of course I did. She was the teacher. She lived under my roof." He shook his head sadly.

"When did you see her last?" Alec asked.

"At dinner, the night before she disappeared."

"Did she seem all right?"

"I remember saying to Eliza after dinner, that girl seems out of sorts. She was playing with her food and upset about something."

"Was that usual?"

"No, no, not at all. We made her part of the family. My wife, the girls, they loved her."

"What happened the day she went missing?"

Charlotte watched Mr. Dredger. "She went off to school in the morning," he said. "She always walked to school with the children. The children came home at the usual time, but she wasn't with them."

"Why didn't you report she was missing? Why didn't you tell me this three weeks ago?"

"I thought she'd run away. Besides, the whole town knew she was missing."

"How did everyone know, Mr. Dredger?"

"Well, she didn't go to school the next day. I rode to the schoolhouse to tell the children to go on home, the teacher wasn't coming."

"All right, so she didn't come home from school. What time was that?"

"I don't rightly know. I was out taking care of the cattle. When I came in for dinner the children were home but Eileen . . ." he paused and cleared his throat. "Miss McArthur wasn't with them."

Alec nodded and paused for a minute. "What did you do?"

"By the time we were finished dinner, it was dark. I went out with a light to guide her in, but I never saw her—not until today."

Alec's tone became very matter of fact. "Do you have any idea who might have wanted to hurt the girl?"

"No one had any reason to want her dead. She was a schoolteacher and a good one. The parents all said the children liked her."

"No one at all?" the sheriff asked.

Mr. Dredger's tone was certain. "No one," he said. "I warned her not to go up the road towards the mines. Often there're miners coming and going on that road. I warned you too, didn't I, girl?" He looked over at Charlotte.

Charlotte's voice was gone and she could only nod.

"Usually it's payday, when they come into town," Alec said.

"Maybe it was Luc Branigan. He's always hanging around these young teachers. And Miss McArthur wasn't showing any interest in anyone. A proud woman, a little standoffish, if you know what I mean."

"Did she go to dances or parties?"

"Nope, not a one. She taught school and went to

the church meetings on Sunday. And she was a big help to Eliza."

"How did Branigan meet her?"

"His brothers and sisters go to the school. Sometimes I'd see him driving her home with the children. He'd drop her where the road turns into my place."

"Why wouldn't he bring her up to the house?"

"Branigan's not welcome on my land. He's a cattle rustler." Mr. Dredger looked like he had a sudden thought. "Maybe the teacher saw something that made her suspicious. Maybe she saw Branigan branding some of my cattle with his mark. Yes, it must have been Branigan. He shot her to keep her quiet."

"I've told you before, Otto, there's no proof that Branigan is a rustler."

"You've never really looked into it, Sheriff."

"Otto, we don't want a range war in these parts. Nothing good ever comes from saying another man is a cattle thief."

"But this is a whole lot more than cattle rustling. It's murder."

Chapter Seventeen

The next morning when Charlotte went into the school, she recognized the box at the front of the room where her desk normally was. It was the box that Straws and Lee had hammered together the night before, Eileen McArthur's coffin.

Guess there wasn't going to be any school today. All of the desks had been moved to one side. Someone had placed the benches around to create rows in front of the coffin.

Charlotte was surprised to see that the lid was off the box. Someone had repaired the damage to Eileen McArthur's clothes, but nothing could be done with the face, which was still a stiff mask. Her coat was securely fastened, not that it would do her much good now.

Charlotte recognized the coat and skirt from the picture in her desk drawer. But where was that lovely hat with the white feather trim? And where was the man who had stood beside her?

The pastor's wife came through the door, carrying a vase of flowers.

She put the vase on the desk beside the coffin. "We're having the funeral here in the schoolroom. It seemed best. This way all the students and their families will be here."

Mrs. Miles looked in the coffin and shook her head disapprovingly. "The children will have nightmares if they see this." She hurried out to find someone to put the top back on.

· · · · ·

The funeral was over and the coffee had been served in the schoolroom. All that was left was to clear away the teacups and serving plates. Most of the women had stayed behind to help, but soon Charlotte and Mrs. Miles were the only ones left.

Charlotte took a deep breath. "There's something I need your help with, Mrs. Miles. I don't want to go back to the Dredger's place."

"What do you want to do?" Mrs. Miles asked.

"I want to live in the teacherage. My contract says the school board will take care of my room and board. It doesn't say that I have to live at the Dredger's."

"Why don't you want to stay there?"

"Yesterday, on the ridge, Mr. Dredger tried to kiss me. He pretended to let me drop over the edge so I would have to hold on to him."

"Are you sure of what you're saying, Charlotte? That's a terrible accusation to make about a married man."

"I know and he's always been kind to me. I feel so confused. And scared. I can't quit this job, Mrs.

Miles. I'm desperate for the money and I don't have anywhere else to go—but I won't stay at the Dredger's. You can talk to the pastor, make him understand."

Mrs. Miles was silent for a minute, and then she sighed. "Eileen McArthur told my husband Mr. Dredger was fresh with her. I couldn't believe it. Otto Dredger is married with children. He is on the school board. Why would he want to be bothering Eileen? My husband told Eileen she must be mistaken. And now she's dead, so we'll never know what really happened."

In silence, they carried the last of the china out to Mrs. Miles's buggy. She climbed up and turned to Charlotte. "I'll arrange a tea with some of the ladies. We'll tell them you need to live in the teacherage to have enough time for your teaching. And I'll get them all to bring some food and supplies. The sheriff is just down the way. I'll get him to look in on you every night. We need to take care of you, Charlotte. We can't lose another teacher."

Chapter Eighteen

Alec Forrest's first stop the next morning was at the train station. He followed Pastor Miles inside. The stationmaster was the only one working so Alec waited while the Pastor bought tickets for the four o'clock train to Missoula on Thanksgiving Day. Then he waited as James Ellis, one of the brothers from the Ellis Mine, made some quiet arrangements about a boxcar with Sam.

Alec wanted to make certain the station was empty so only Sam Wilberforce heard his questions.

"Has Luc Branigan shipped any cattle recently?"

"Yes, about two weeks ago."

"Did you see the brands?"

"Why are you asking?" Wilberforce wanted to know.

"It's possible the teacher, Miss McArthur, saw him rebranding cattle."

"You don't think he killed her?" The stationmaster sounded skeptical.

"Just investigating, Sam."

Wilberforce had a serious expression on his face. "Branigan did ship some cattle, but it was after the teacher went missing. Four of them were calves, and yes, he might have put the Branigan brand over Dredger's brand. It was impossible to be sure, Sheriff, and we shipped the cattle out that afternoon."

Alec knew that Sam would not want to accuse a man directly. This conversation was about done. "Oh, that sounds bad for Luc," was all he said.

Alec went over to the jail to get his deputy. The two men rode out towards the Dredger place and then cut back on the road through Branigan land. None of the land was fenced, and by the law of the open range, cattle were free to roam.

They rode along the creek and found a recent campfire. Someone had blazed a log with a Lazy B, the Branigan brand. Luc Branigan had been here branding cattle. Alec and his deputy looked around the site. In the trees, close to the campfire they found a navy blue hat. After a month outside, the feathers on that hat were pretty battered but they were still white.

They rode on to the Branigan ranch house. They found Luc in a barn. Alec had the blue hat in one hand.

"You recognize this, Luc?"

Luc looked at it for a moment. "That's the teacher's hat. Miss McArthur's hat."

"We found it on your land. Over near the ford where you've been branding. Recently. When did you see Miss McArthur last?"

Luc hesitated before he replied. Then he said, "I saw her the day she disappeared. She was on the main street walking towards the edge of town."

"Why was she walking, Luc? I thought you or

one of your men usually picked up her and the children after school."

"She told me she would rather walk."

"Why would she rather walk than get a ride back to the ranch?" Alec had a feeling in his gut that something had happened between Luc and the teacher.

"What are you saying, Sheriff?"

"Luc, this links you to her death."

. . . . .

Wednesday morning, in the classroom, Charlotte listened to the stillness. For once, she didn't feel rushed. Her classroom was organized for the day. The assignments for each grade were on the blackboard, so everyone could get busy as soon as school started. They would spend the morning doing reading and math and the afternoon rehearsing for the Thanksgiving Pageant. By now, all the children should know their lines.

She lifted the brass box out of the bottom drawer of her desk. She ran her fingers over the smooth finish and thought for a minute about the woman who had owned it. What an awful way to die, shot in the woods, her body lying in a frozen stream for over a month.

The door at the back of the classroom opened and a man appeared in the doorway. He was dressed in heavy canvas pants, a knit shirt and suspenders. A miner.

"You're the man in the picture," Charlotte said.

"Who are you?" the man asked.

"I'm Charlotte Fraser, the teacher here. This is my classroom."

"Your classroom? Where's Eileen McArthur?"

"You knew her," Charlotte said. It was a statement, not a question.

"Of course I did. What's going on here?"

"Please calm down, Mr . . .?" She raised her voice.

"Neil McArthur."

"Oh, my goodness." It was all that she could say.

"She's my wife," Neil said.

"I didn't know she was married." Charlotte was astonished.

"I came as soon as I got her letter. Where is she?" Charlotte recognized the letter in his hand. It was the one Charlotte had mailed the first day of school.

She wished there were anybody else here to give Neil this news. Very gently, she said, "Eileen is dead. Her funeral was yesterday. You've only just missed it."

Neil McArthur's eyes went wide with shock. "What happened to her?"

"I could go and get the sheriff. I'm sure he'll want to talk to you." She went outside. Tommy Dredger was playing in the schoolyard. She sent him to get the sheriff and went back inside to wait with Neil McArthur.

"She wanted to leave," Neil said "She wanted to leave, but I told her to stay. It's no life for a woman out on a gold claim. And she was making good money here."

There was nothing Charlotte could say.

"She was afraid of something. Everyone here thought she was single and there aren't very many single women in Bandit Creek," Neil said.

"I have some of her things," Charlotte said. "She left them here in the desk."

She pushed the brass box with the picture and letters across to him. Then she lifted the gold locket out of the bottom of the drawer.

"Is there a wallet?" Neil asked.

"This is everything I have. Anything else must be in her trunk at the Dredger's."

The gold locket spun around on the chain when Charlotte passed it to him. "Eileen wrote me about that locket," Neil said as he reached for it. "Someone must have given it to her."

Charlotte noticed a thistle carved into the back of the locket, and pulled it back to take a closer look. "Was Eileen Scottish?"

"No, her family name was Devlin."

"I saw a watch with the exact same carving of a thistle," Charlotte said. She thought about Otto Dredger's watch. Then she remembered Eliza Dredger searching under the sofa for something.

Neil took the locket from her. "Pretty little thing," he said. He took the picture out of the locket and examined it.

"This here is Laura Wallace," he said, surprise in his voice.

"Who is Laura Wallace?" Alec asked from the back of the room.

"She was a teacher, back in Galveston. She taught both of us, Eileen and me. We grew up near Galveston. Laura's dad owned a big ranch. They all died during a hurricane. Their ranch hands said they were murdered."

"Why did Eileen have that locket?"

"I don't know, Sheriff. In her last letter, she said she was afraid and wanted me to come and get her. I came as soon as I got the letter."

"When did you see her last?" Alec asked.

"It was about a month ago. I used to come to town to see her, but we didn't want anyone to suspect she was married, so we met up on a ledge above the river."

"Over by the waterfalls?" asked Charlotte.

"Yes, you can see for miles around up there."

"How did you know about that ledge?" Charlotte asked. "You really can't see it from the top of the cliff."

"Eileen said she'd been there before."

"Could I see that locket?" Alec asked. Neil handed it over.

Alec turned the locket in his hand. "I would like

to keep the locket," Alec said. "It could be a clue to who killed her."

"Eileen had a little wallet," Neil said again. "It has all of my wages from the mine. I didn't want to keep the money on me."

"Check with Otto Dredger," Alec said. "That's where she was boarding."

Charlotte pictured Otto Dredger in her mind, pulling the gold chain and ring from Eileen McArthur's body and wondered whether Neil McArthur would ever get his money.

"Can you think of anyone who might have harmed your wife?" Alec asked.

"There was one fellow who was a rancher who kept asking her to go riding with him. She was trying to keep our marriage a secret, so she went out riding with him a few times."

"Did she tell you a name?"

"Someone named Luc, Luc Branigan, I think she said. She told me she was going to have to tell him to leave her alone."

"Is that who she was afraid of?"

"She didn't say in her letter, just that she had a locket with a picture in it. Something wasn't right and I had to come for her."

After Neil left, Alec stayed behind. "We're holding Luc Branigan for the murder. I hope that makes you feel safer."

"I can't believe Luc killed her," Charlotte said. "He's been so good to me."

"He's been rebranding some of Otto Dredger's cattle as Branigan cattle. I think Eileen McArthur saw him. And we found her hat near his campfire."

"He used to pick us up at school and drive us home," Charlotte said. "He seemed so nice."

Alec looked at her carefully. "Are you fond of Luc?" he asked.

. . . . .

That night Charlotte had her dinner in the teacherage. She cleaned up the dishes, made a cup of tea, and sat down. She ate one of the cookies that the ladies had left for her. She listened to the silence. It was the first time she had ever had a place of her own. She could hardly believe it, and it felt wonderful.

Charlotte saw Alec walk by the window and heard his knock on the door. She smoothed her dress and hair, and she let him in.

"Are you really going to come and check on me every night?" she asked.

"Mrs. Miles would have my head, if I didn't," Alec said ruefully.

"Does Mrs. Miles run this town?"

"It's best to let her think she does. Then everyone can get about their business. Besides, a young woman living here by yourself, I like to know you're safe, too."

"I can take care of myself," Charlotte said, thinking of the revolver in her purse.

He smiled. "You certainly aren't the helpless type."

"I'm glad you came by, Sheriff. I need to talk to you about that locket that Eileen McArthur had. Otto Dredger has a pocket watch with that same thistle engraved on it. Same as the locket. He had a picture of a girl and he said it was his sister, Laura. I don't believe him."

"Neil McArthur was pretty sure that girl in the locket was Laura Wallace," Alec said. "I sent a telegram to the Galveston sheriff to find out what happened to her and her family."

. . . . .

Annie Hamilton was getting ready for her first visitor on the following Tuesday evening. When he got there, Pastor Miles was out of breath because his wife had been late leaving for her meeting. But he had the train tickets for Annie and her son.

After they made love, they lay together in silence for a few minutes. Then he said, "I'll be so glad to take you away from all this."

"Not nearly as happy as me."

"I want to go to the train separately," he said. "In case my wife decides to come and see me off. There's no point in embarrassing her."

She took the tickets from him. "Separate is fine."

The pastor left so he would be home well before his wife. In that minute, Annie knew the pastor was never going to leave Mabel. He might think so, but when he was settled in Seattle, she would join him. Some things never changed.

Annie tucked the tickets away before Otto Dredger came up the stairs. They made plans about picking Tommy up on Thanksgiving. Otto agreed that Annie could take him from school after the pageant. They would have plenty of time before the train left. For once, she felt the prospect of happiness. She could only hope that Dredger wouldn't change his mind.

Otto wanted to talk about the new teacher. Had Pastor Miles said anything about why she moved into the teacherage?

"The pastor said that Miss Fraser was looking for more time to prepare for her classes and was busy getting ready for Thanksgiving. She is dedicated to her work."

He wasn't satisfied, but went on, "Do you think Luc Branigan killed Miss McArthur?"

"Nobody seems to believe Luc did it," she told him, "It certainly is a mystery. Although Miss Fraser found a locket in the classroom, and the sheriff thinks it might be a clue to the murder."

Otto lost control. "Branigan is a rustler and a murderer," he shouted and stormed out.

· · · · ·

Charlotte was getting ready for bed when she heard some noises on the breezeway outside her door. She got back into her clothes and lit her lantern before she ventured outside.

Across the breezeway, the door to the classroom hung open. "Is anybody there?" Charlotte called out. She could hear someone tearing through things in the classroom, looking for something. She backed away from the door and closed it securely behind her. Then she propped her single chair against it.

· · · · ·

The next morning, Charlotte stayed in the teacherage until she could hear children gathering in the schoolyard. She went outside and asked one of the boys to run and get the sheriff before she crossed over to the schoolroom.

The schoolroom had been torn apart. The desks were turned over and books and papers littered the floor. The books from the bookcase were thrown at the back of the room. The intruder had dumped the contents of her desk on the floor. The costumes for the Thanksgiving Pageant were flung around everywhere.

Alec came in, looked around and led Charlotte outside. She followed him without speaking. He told the children there wouldn't be any school today and went next door to the church. He asked Pastor Miles to come and take charge of getting the children home.

"What am I going to do with you?" he asked Charlotte.

"I'll be fine. But who would want to do this to a schoolroom?"

"They were obviously looking for something," Alec said.

· · · · ·

The following morning, it was school as usual. Charlotte spent the morning doing lessons with the children and in the afternoon, they had a huge group effort to replace the costumes that had been wrecked.

At the end of the day, Maud Dredger came up to Charlotte's desk. The little girl was excited. She had a new brother, and her mother wanted Charlotte to come out to the ranch to see baby Adam.

Chapter Nineteen

Charlotte was exhausted by the end of the week. The days flew by as she worked with her class and got to know the students better. The evenings, alone in the teacherage, were hard, and Charlotte worried about whether she would have another midnight visitor. She awaited Alec's nightly calls so she could assure him she was all right and then go to bed. But sleep eluded her. She knew she was overreacting to the break-in, but still she could not shake a nagging fear.

She had the luxury of staying in bed well after daybreak on Saturday morning. She wanted to do a little shopping to get a gift for baby Adam.

After lunch, she set out for the ranch, gift in hand. She missed the horses from the ranch, but the day was cold and clear and she walked briskly to get there. When she arrived, the kids were happy to see her and Maud even made tea for her and Eliza.

Baby Adam was gorgeous. He had fine blond hair that formed tiny curls, like his father. His eyes were ice blue and Charlotte adored the little guy. It seemed like his sisters did as well. Tommy, on the other hand, was not so impressed, but then what could you expect from an older brother?

The afternoon passed quickly and before Charlotte realized it, the clock in the hall was chiming four o'clock. She had to leave if she was going to get back before dark.

Tommy came with her and they walked along the road towards the bridge. He seemed to be in a serious mood and then he asked her, "Do you like it here, Miss Fraser?"

"I do, Tommy. I love teaching and I love the children in the class. Why do you ask?"

"I liked Miss McArthur, and I miss her. Are you going to leave too?"

"I hope I'll stay a long time."

"I hope so, too. You know who my real mother is. And you can keep my secret."

Oh, my, gosh. Charlotte didn't know what to say to the boy. They walked on in silence. Finally she said, "Is it hard, keeping this secret?"

"I can keep secrets. I wish I didn't have to."

She felt sorry for him. "What secrets are hard, Tommy?"

"My dad told me a secret about Miss McArthur. But then she was dead."

That was strange. "Where is your dad today, Tommy?" Mr. Dredger had been on the back of her mind all day.

"He's up on Crow Mountain. He's going to blast out some stumps. He wants me to help."

"You're too young to be helping to blast out stumps."

"That's what my mom says."

Charlotte almost asked him which mother, but

she bit her tongue. When they got to the bridge, Charlotte sent Tommy back.

The sun was setting behind Crow Mountain and Charlotte looked up to watch it. A band of pink light lit up the mountain peaks. She enjoyed the sound of the water splashing on the ice-covered rocks below her. She took a deep breath to release the fear she'd been feeling all week.

The main road to town was around the next bend in the trail. The sounds from the creek disappeared and Charlotte was alert to the sudden quiet around her. She heard the creaking of twigs behind her in the bush. She imagined a bear or a cougar and started making as much noise as she possibly could. She began to run.

Once she reached the main road, she slowed and looked back to see if anything, or anyone, came out of the woods. Thankfully, she was alone. She kept up a quick pace into town and, back at the teacherage, closed and locked the door behind her.

She was especially happy to have Alec Forrest come by to check on her that night.

Chapter Twenty

On the day before Thanksgiving, after the dress rehearsal, Charlotte picked up two letters from the post office, one from Ora and one from Gilbert.

Ora's letter was filled with news about plans for her wedding. Ora closed by saying how much she wished Charlotte were going to be there. Then she wrote that she understood why Charlotte had left. It would be the closest thing to an apology Charlotte would ever get from Ora.

Charlotte read the letter over a couple of times. It sounded exactly the way Ora spoke. Charlotte and Ora had been best friends forever and Charlotte missed her. But Charlotte knew they would never be that close again. She remembered when Ora announced her engagement to Gilbert. It had been a blind side for Charlotte but Ora was so excited, so radiant. Maybe Ora had always loved Gilbert.

The second letter was from Gilbert. Charlotte's first love. She had been devastated over the engagement. Charlotte wondered what on earth he had to say to her.

She didn't have the courage to read the letter yet. She needed to be with someone she could trust. And she knew just who that person was.

. . . . .

Alec Forrest answered the knock, and found Charlotte standing on his doorstep. He backed away from his front door, not knowing what to say.

"I thought I would come by before you came to check up on me."

"You are always surprising me, Charlotte."

"It's a sad night for me. I didn't want to be alone."

He let her in.

"May I play the piano for a bit?"

"No one ever plays it much. I'm happy to listen to you play."

While she played, he got up and poured himself a glass of whiskey. His mother had loved the piano. For a few minutes, he allowed himself the indulgence of missing her.

"Play the Oldsmobile song," he said when Charlotte paused. She found the music and began.

When Charlotte finished the song she turned to him and asked, very seriously, "Do you think it's possible, if you lose everyone you love, to ever love again?"

It was like she'd read his mind. Silence. She pointed to the whiskey "I'd like a glass, too, if I may." He nodded, and poured her a glass.

"Luc Branigan tried to kiss me at that dance. And when he did, I was comparing him to Gilbert."

"Who's Gilbert?" Alec had to know.

"Gilbert was my boyfriend."

"You have a boyfriend?" There was alarm in his voice.

"Before my parents moved to California, he was calling on me. I told everyone that I stayed behind because I wanted to go to Normal School. But the truth of it was, I wouldn't leave Gilbert."

"And then you left him anyway? Why?"

"He's getting married tomorrow. On Thanksgiving. To my best friend, Ora. That's why I came out here."

She took a drink. "I gave up my family for him. Mr. Sharp lent me the money to go to Normal School, so that's why I had to get a job."

"How old are you?"

"Probably eighteen," she said. "Maybe seventeen. My mom can't remember for certain what year I was born."

"You'll find someone else. Any man would be happy to have you."

"Any man?"

"Any man," he repeated. She got up and settled into the sofa beside him.

She pulled the letter out of her pocket. "Gilbert sent me a letter. I got it today. I haven't wanted to open it."

He took the letter from her. "What if he said it was all a mistake and that he wants you back?"

"I never want to see him again. I have a new life here."

"What if he just wants to apologize?"

"I hope that's what he wrote, but still…." She watched the flames in the fireplace. This was a cozy room. She liked this man. "I don't need to read this. It won't change anything." She went over and dropped the letter in the fire. It smoldered for a moment and then exploded in flames.

"Would you play the song again?" he asked.

She sat down at the piano and picked out the tune. It was a cheerful melody, and she sang along with it.

She got up and sank into the sofa beside him. "The thing is, I don't want to have to wake up every Thanksgiving and think this is the day that Gilbert married Ora. Give me something else to remember."

"You're playing with fire, Charlotte. And you could have anyone. Someone with a proper job who can be a family man."

"I think you're the one."

Chapter Twenty-One

At home in the teacherage, Charlotte sat in her one chair, arms wrapped around her legs. Alec had kissed her. She could tell he was as inexperienced as she was. And nervous, very, very nervous. They had shared another glass of the whiskey that everyone in Bandit Creek seemed to drink. He had moved slowly, building up the fire until it reached a roaring blaze. She was more than ready to make love to him, but it wasn't to be.

"We need to stop now, Charlotte. Otherwise, I don't know what will happen."

She found this hard to believe.

"It's time I take you home. I've seen enough young girls get into trouble in this town. I won't be responsible for anything like that happening to you."

He walked her back to the teacherage. And then he was gone.

. . . . .

Alec barely finished breakfast before the deputy knocked on the front door.

"There was a miner found dead in the creek yesterday, five miles down from town. They're saying the dead man is Neil McArthur, the dead teacher's husband."

"We should have gone out there as soon as we heard about it."

"I knew you'd say that. That's why I waited until this morning to tell you."

. . . . .

Today was Thanksgiving. Charlotte put all of her questions about Alec out of her mind and crossed over to the school. There were already children milling around in the schoolyard. She got some of the big boys to come in and help her set up the classroom. Then she helped all the children into their costumes, bonnets and hats for the Pilgrims, headdresses and beads for the natives.

Nellie Welch ran over to Charlotte in tears. Her Indian princess dress was missing. The dress had been in the schoolroom last night. Charlotte guessed that one of the other little girls must have been jealous of the dress. She gathered all the girls into a circle and said, "This pageant is for all of you and all of your parents. We can't disappoint them. Each of you take one part of the room, look in the desks, and look in the coatroom. We'll find Nellie's dress for certain."

The little girls went off to search, and a few minutes later Nellie's dress miraculously emerged from behind the boot rack in the coatroom.

Charlotte took a deep breath. It looked as if everything was ready. But where was Tommy Dredger? His headdress was sitting on his desk. Charlotte asked Maud where her brother was.

"He had to go out and help Dad today," Maud said. "Dad is blasting stumps out in the upper pasture."

"But he can't miss the Thanksgiving Pageant."

"We all told Dad, and Tommy even cried, but Daddy said he was old enough to start earning his keep." It looked like Maud was going to start crying. Charlotte patted the little girl's back.

Then she called Dylan Branigan over and told him he had to play Tommy's part as Squanto, the Indian who taught the Pilgrims how to plant corn. The show must go on.

She settled the feather headdress on Dylan's head, covering his bright red hair. "You'll do fine, Dylan. I know you've memorized everybody's lines."

Dylan Branigan looked up at her and grinned. Charlotte felt like she was looking at a ghost. Dylan had the exact same brown eyes as Tommy Dredger. He could be Tommy's brother . . . or uncle.

When all of the parents were seated in the schoolroom, and it was time for the show, Charlotte took the children out to the cloakroom and gathered them together. "Good luck, everyone. All you have to do is speak up and say your lines clearly, just like we practiced."

Charlotte led the Indians to the front of the classroom to begin the pageant. Then the Pilgrims made their entrance, sliding the Mayflower along the floor to the front of the room. Charlotte stood off to the side. There was nothing more for her to do but enjoy the play.

For the most part, the children delivered their lines flawlessly. The natives welcomed the Pilgrims to America and the Pilgrims gave thanks for the land and freedom from persecution. Dylan Branigan delivered his lines as Squanto.

Then the smallest children came to the front of the room, dressed as the corn and the turkey and pumpkin. The little ones only managed to stand and wave at their parents. Then one of the older girls whispered their lines to them and they all said them together.

Finally, the children sang Turkey in the Straw and took a bow. To close things off, Pastor Miles led a prayer of Thanksgiving for the harvest, the success of the mines, and for the opportunity to live in America.

The pageant over, Charlotte was surrounded by parents congratulating her on the program. Mrs. Miles and some of the ladies served coffee and then Mrs. Miles stayed behind to help Charlotte clean up.

"There's no need for me to hurry home, dear," she said. "Mr. Miles is taking the four o'clock train today. It's still a secret, but he's been offered a parish in Seattle."

"You must be excited," Charlotte said. "You'll be living in a big city. There's always so much more to see and to do."

"Well, no. It will be a wonderful opportunity for Mr. Miles. A bigger church, a bigger congregation, a bigger choir. As for me, I don't want to go. I get tired out with all the moving around a minister has to do. We always need to decorate a new house and make new friends."

"Don't you find that exciting?"

"Not anymore, I don't. I hope he goes and checks it out, changes his mind and comes back."

"But what will you do if he loves it there?"

"I hope he doesn't. Every congregation has its own problems, people who like to feel they are in charge of everything."

Charlotte smiled to herself.

"Yes, I know what you're thinking. I do like to help my husband organize his duties. He's such a caring, gentle soul. If I didn't take care of things around here, people would walk all over him."

"Well, you've been a huge help to me. Helping me to move into the teacherage. Getting the ladies to send over food and supplies. And to think, a month ago, we were strangers."

"And now I really feel like we are friends," Mrs. Miles said.

"I'm surprised you don't have children of you own."

"We tried, when we were first married. But we

lost our babies, you see, and then we just stopped trying."

"I'm sorry to hear that."

Mrs. Miles sighed. "We never know what the future holds for us, Charlotte. We've got to accept our lot and make the best of things."

The two women worked in silence.

Charlotte realized that never once had she thought about Gilbert after Alec had taken her in his arms. But was she in love with Alec or was she simply trying to forget about Gilbert? Was she hurting Alec to make herself feel better?

Annie Hamilton burst into the room. For a moment, Charlotte didn't recognize her. Annie was dressed in a black dress with a matching wrap. Not her usual vivid colors, the ones she liked to draw attention to herself.

Mrs. Miles stiffened. Annie's eyes widened at the sight of Mrs. Miles, but she didn't acknowledge the woman in any manner.

"Charlotte, I need to talk to you," Annie said.

Mrs. Miles interrupted. "What are you doing here? If I could give you some advice, Miss Hamilton, you should leave your sinful ways behind you and find a decent job."

"Answer me one question," Annie said. "Who in this town would give me a decent job?"

Mrs. Miles didn't have an answer. She ignored Annie and started to collect some cups and saucers, banging them noisily as she put them away.

"Where's Tommy, Charlotte?" Annie asked. "I was waiting for him but I never saw him leave."

Charlotte bit her lower lip. "Tommy wasn't here for the pageant. Mr. Dredger said Tommy's old enough to be earning his keep and took him out to work with him."

"But I pay . . ."Annie stopped herself. "Today's the day the gold shipment is coming in. Dredger should be trying to see the Ellis brothers. Do you know where Dredger and Tommy are?"

"They went to the upper pasture. Maud said Mr. Dredger wants to blast some stumps out up there this afternoon."

"Tommy? Help him with dynamite? The man's a fool. He's going to kill that boy." Her anger disappeared and her face went faint. "Oh my God. He wants to kill Tommy." Lines of fear crossed her face and her hands trembled.

Charlotte could not believe what the woman was saying. "Why would he want to kill Tommy?"

"I think Dredger killed Eileen McArthur. I saw Tommy ahead of her on the road on the day she went missing. Tommy knows something about that day and he told me his father wanted him to keep a secret."

She walked over and flung a train ticket at Mrs. Miles. "I'm going to get Tommy. I'll never make that four o'clock train. As for you, you old fool, you should be on that train to Missoula. And if I could give you some advice, you might spend a little more time taking care of your husband and a little less time having tea with the church ladies."

Annie turned to Charlotte. "Please go and find Sheriff Forrest. I saw him heading over towards Chinatown. Tell him that Dredger is planning to rob the gold shipment."

"How could you know that?"

"I don't have time to explain. Just tell the sheriff. The gold shipment is on the way from Crow Mountain to the train this afternoon. I have to find Tommy." And she hurried out the door.

. . . . .

Annie paused outside the jail. Luc Branigan had to be inside.

The jail was empty except for Luc.

"Where is everyone?" Annie asked.

"The sheriff went out. There's been some trouble he had to see about. As soon as he left, the deputy said he was going up to Crow Mountain for the afternoon."

The key for the lockup was on a hook behind the sheriff's desk. Annie grabbed it and opened the door.

Luc touched the sleeve of the black dress she was wearing. "Good heavens, Annie, you look like the preacher's wife. Did you take my advice and give up whoring?"

She wanted to slap the smug smile off his face but instead she said, "I need your help, Luc."

He smiled down at her. "I always was a pushover for a lady in need."

"Otto Dredger has Tommy with him, up on the mountain. They're getting ready to set off some dynamite. I'm afraid he's going to kill Tommy."

"Why would Dredger kill his own kid?"

Now was not the time for this conversation. "I need your help, Luc. Please."

"What do you want me to do?"

"Ride up there with me. Save Tommy."

"What makes you think Dredger would kill the boy?"

"He's a murderer, Luc."

"He's been coming up to see you every Tuesday for the past four years. I warned you about him and now, after all this time, you say he's a murderer?"

"Luc, did you kill Eileen McArthur?"

"How can you even ask me that?"

"If you didn't kill her, then who did?"

"Annie, it could have been anybody. It could have been a miner she was meeting. I saw them meeting up on Dredger's ledge."

"No one can see that ledge. Dredger told me."

"I can see it from the ridge on my land, Annie."

"Oh, Luc. Is that how you knew Dredger and I had been together?"

"Annie, I don't want to talk about that. All I'm saying is, it could have been that miner who killed

Miss McArthur."

"Luc, please, I'm begging you. I need your help to save Tommy."

"Do you want to talk about it? How you walked all over my heart? How you went from me to Dredger in two days."

"All right, Luc, I made a mistake. Does it make you happy to hear me admit it? I was young and didn't know any better."

"No, it doesn't make me happy."

She had to make him understand. "Luc, Tommy told me that Dredger was making him keep a secret about Eileen McArthur. He never told me what it was. But I think Tommy is the one person who knows who killed her."

"Why don't you tell the sheriff and let him take care of it?" Luc demanded.

"Tommy is my son, Luc. And he's your son. And Dredger is going to kill him because of it."

· · · · ·

Luc Branigan wasn't going anywhere with Annie Hamilton. He stopped by the Powder Horn for a drink. Eventually the sheriff would find out he wasn't in jail and come looking for him.

Damn that woman. Tommy was his son? That was possible. Damn her. He couldn't let her go after Dredger on her own, but he would be damned if he was going with her.

JD had been sitting over in the corner by himself. "Will you buy me a drink, Luc?" the old man asked. Luc gestured at the bartender and he poured Jack a shot. Luc could swear that man was a ghost.

Jack sipped the whiskey slowly. He relaxed back into his chair, lost for a moment in some world of his own. Then he had a lucid moment. "Don't let her go up on Crow Mountain alone, Luc. You'll never be able to live with yourself."

"I have a hard enough time living with myself now, old man." He downed his drink and went out to find Annie.

· · · · ·

Charlotte started her search for Alec at the Chinese laundry but he had gone over to the Powder Horn, to settle some fight.

Charlotte gritted her teeth and walked through the swinging doors of the saloon.

The bartender told her the sheriff had gone upstairs to see a couple of the dance girls who had been fighting. Charlotte ignored the catcalls as she climbed up the staircase to the second floor.

Down in Annie's room, two girls were picking through Annie's things.

"What's going on?" Charlotte asked.

"Annie is leaving. Two of the girls got into a fight about some of the things she left behind."

"Where's the sheriff?"

"After he broke up the fight, he went down the back way. One of the girls had a knife. The sheriff took the other girl to the doctor's office."

Charlotte went down the back way herself. She didn't want to go through the saloon again.

Charlotte ran back to Alec's house and let herself in the back door. She knew his Oldsmobile was in the old shed at the back. The engine turned over the second time she tried to start it. She backed it out and drove over to the doctor's place.

Alec was coming out of the doctor's office when Charlotte drove up. He turned his head to one side.

"Did I say you could drive my car?"

"I needed it to find you. Annie says Otto Dredger is going to rob some Ellis gold this afternoon."

Alec walked around the car and got in. "There is a gold shipment coming in today from the Ellis Mine. Going out on the four o'clock train. Take me back to the office and then take my car back home. Where's Annie now?"

"She was going up to the mountain to try to save Tommy. She thinks Otto Dredger's going to kill him."

"Why would he do that?"

"Annie thinks Tommy knows who killed Eileen McArthur. She thinks it was Dredger."

"I was sure Annie knew more than she was saying."

"What will we do?"

"We? There's no we. I'll go up the mountain and sort out what's going on."

"I could help."

"You could help by going back to the teacherage and barricading the door. Or go over to Pastor Miles's place and stay with them. Or drive my car home and lock yourself in my place."

"I could help you," she repeated.

"I saw my parents being shot. I don't want to repeat the experience with you. Stop here," he said when they reached the deputy's house.

Alec disappeared inside for a minute and then came out.

"His wife said Frank is up on Crow Mountain, hunting. Thanksgiving is an odd day to go hunting." He stopped to think.

He looked at his watch. "It's almost one o'clock. The gold shipment should be coming in soon. Take me by the stables and then go home. My home. Where did you learn to drive?"

"My dad had a truck on the farm. I used to deliver milk every day to the Chinese restaurant in town."

"A woman riding astride. Driving my car." He shook his head sadly. "This whole world is changing too fast for me."

"You sound old when you say that."

"My mother always said I was an old soul trapped in a young body."

Chapter Twenty-Two

Luc Branigan led the way along the ridge of Crow Mountain. He and Annie were on horseback. They spotted Dredger, in among the trees and rode down towards him.

Dredger looked up. "Annie, what are you doing out here?"

"I came to get Tommy. I'm taking him with me today."

"No, Annie, you're not. I'm getting ready to blast some stumps. I need him to help me. And best you two get out of here. You don't want to be hurt when this dynamite blows."

Branigan looked around. "This isn't pasture land, Dredger. Just let us take the boy and go."

Dredger laughed. "I don't think so, Branigan. You're not taking my son."

"Otto, please. You promised me I could take him," Annie said.

"You always were a fool who believed what you wanted to hear, Annie. I'm keeping Tommy here."

In the distance, they could see Tommy setting sticks of dynamite into holes along the ridge. Annie rode her horse towards the boy.

Dredger pulled a revolver out of his saddlebag and fired a single shot in the air. Annie pulled up on her horse and looked around. The revolver was aimed directly at her.

"Don't make me take a second shot, Annie. Leave now."

"We're not going anywhere without the boy," Branigan said.

"You're a fool, Branigan. Turn back and nobody will get hurt."

Tommy ran towards his mother. "Now, that is just too bad," Dredger said.

Frank, the deputy, rode up the trail. "What's going on?"

"Things are getting out of control," Dredger said. "You were supposed to watch the trail and make sure no one came up."

"Nobody rode by me. Annie, what are you doing up here?"

"Getting my son. Tommy's my boy."

"You can't leave now," Dredger said. "We have a job to do, and we don't want you stirring up trouble."

"What are we going to do, Otto?" the deputy asked.

"We'll put them on the ledge under the cliff. We'll tie them up and then after we finish the job, we'll let them go."

"I don't like this," Frank said. "Nobody is supposed to get hurt."

"Nobody will get hurt, Frank. We'll take the gold and then they'll be free to go."

Frank didn't reply.

"In for a penny, in for pound," Dredger said. "There's some rope over with my things. Tie them up and put them down on the ledge. Nobody will see them there."

Frank nodded slowly.

"You're not taking me anywhere," Branigan said.

Dredger looked Luc straight in the eye and shot him in his left leg. "I'll kill you like I killed your father, Branigan. But first I'll kill Annie if you give me any more trouble."

· · · · ·

Alec got Charlotte to stop at the jail. He picked up a shotgun and strapped it on his hip beside his police revolver. Luc was gone, but he would have to wait until later. Right now, he had to go and find out what was happening on Crow Mountain.

· · · · ·

Charlotte returned the Oldsmobile to Alec's shed and let herself in his house. She went to the window that had a view of Crow Mountain. Dredger's ranch was around on the backside of the mountain and all she could see was rock and snow and sky.

Through the window, she saw the stationmaster come up the path to the house. She went to the door to tell him the sheriff wasn't home.

"I have a telegram for the sheriff from Galveston, Texas. Do you know where he is?"

"He's gone up to Crow Mountain. There's some trouble with Dredger."

"All the more reason he gets this, Miss Fraser. He needs to see it as soon as possible."

"Give it to me, Mr. Wilberforce. I'll be sure he gets it."

The stationmaster left and, of course, Charlotte opened the telegram. Laura Wallace and her family had been murdered the night of the Galveston hurricane. The main suspect was a young cowboy from the area, Otto Dredger. He had never been located or arrested. If he was being held in Bandit Creek, the sheriff in Galveston wanted to be notified.

· · · · ·

Charlotte sped down the road out of town, and turned off at the Branigan place. The Oldsmobile was an old car, but it still had a lot of power. Charlotte was not familiar with the old mining roads leading up to the cliffs, so she just kept turning towards the creek. She knew the exact place Dredger would choose to attack the shipment, right where the cliff overhung the road to the mine.

The road was barely more than a track through

the trees. It curved sharply, led across a meadow and went up a steep ridge.

She stopped the car at the top beside a row of trees. The trees blocked her view of the Dredger place.

She walked through the trees to the top of the rise, where she could see directly across the creek to the road that led to the mine. The cliff towered above the road, and she could see Tommy sitting on a ledge below the cliff, legs hanging over the side.

With a start, she recognized the ledge as the one Otto Dredger had taken her to, the day they went out riding. He didn't know it was so visible.

Charlotte could make out the Deputy, Frank, beside Tommy. Behind them were two other people, Annie Hamilton, in a black dress bending over someone else who was on the ledge. Something must be wrong because the man was lying prone on the earth.

Charlotte spotted Alec Forrest as he climbed along the cliff from the north. He wouldn't be able to see the people below him on the ledge.

Mr. Dredger was the only one on the top of the cliff when Alec broke out of the trees and approached him. Charlotte could see the two men talking. Then Alec was walking about, checking out something on the edge of the cliff.

As Alec leaned over to pick something up, Dredger approached him from behind, a gun in his hand. Charlotte shouted out a warning, but her voice was lost in the wind.

Time stood still as Charlotte watched Dredger creep up on the sheriff. Alec turned in Dredger's direction and Dredger shot him.

Alec fell, his shotgun falling to the ground beside him. Then Dredger dragged him to the edge of the cliff and rolled him over the edge. Charlotte stared in shock. His body dropped about ten feet, to the ledge below.

Dredger took Alec's shotgun and fastened it to the back of his saddle. Then Charlotte saw him pull his pocket watch out of his vest and check the time.

Charlotte ran to the car, and drove back as fast as she could along the bumpy tracks.

Chapter Twenty-Three

Dredger checked the dynamite in the holes along the face of the cliff and then he looked at his watch again. He still had an hour before the gold shipment was due to appear. Everything was in place even though these idiots had tried to interfere with his plans. Too bad Annie and Branigan and the sheriff had come up onto his property and stuck their noses into his business, but he would take care of them. No stone would be left unturned at the end of this day. He smiled at his own joke.

· · · · ·

Alec landed heavily onto the ledge. A few bushes softened his fall, but the force of the drop sent pain shooting through his body. He saw Luc and Annie, and then he passed out.

· · · · ·

Alec gradually became aware of someone shaking him. His deputy, Frank.

"Sheriff, are you okay?"

Alec shook his head. He could move his arms

and his legs but the warm blood spreading across his chest was a bad sign. "Can't you see I've been shot? What are you doing up here, Frank?"

The deputy gave him a look of despair. "I didn't know what I was getting into. Otto Dredger hired me for the day to keep people away from the cliff while he was doing some blasting. Nobody was supposed to get hurt. Now Dredger is going and shooting people."

"Who else did he shoot?"

Frank gestured over at Luc Branigan. Alec pulled himself up on one arm to look. Luc was lying on the ledge. Annie Hamilton was bent over him and the boy, Tommy, was close by her side.

Frank made a bandage out of his bandana and tied it against the wound on Alec's chest.

"Dredger shot Luc. And he said he shot Branigan's father. I bandaged Luc up, but he needs to see a doctor. So do you."

"We need to get off this ledge," Annie said.

The deputy continued, "Dredger wanted me to tie everybody up and put them on this ledge, but I didn't. Annie helped me to get Luc down here and now we're just waiting to see what Dredger is going to do."

"What is Dredger doing up here?" Alec asked.

Annie answered. "He wants to rob the gold shipment coming from the mine today."

Frank nodded his head.

Tommy looked scared. "No, he's not. He is

blasting to make a pasture."

Otto Dredger came to the top of the path leading down to the ridge.

"What's going on, Dad?" Tommy asked. "I saw you shoot Luc. What happened to the sheriff?"

"Everything's okay, son. It was an accident when Luc got shot."

"Stay here, Tommy," Annie said. The boy sat back beside his mother.

"Recognize this place, Annie?" Otto Dredger asked. Annie winced.

From his position on the ground, Alec watched Dredger. The man looked confident. "This is where I brought Annie, the first time—the first time I had her. Right on that rock, right where you're lying now, Branigan. Annie and me. I was just sad to find out someone else had her first. I always suspected that someone was you, Branigan."

Otto looked at Annie. "So when you turned out to be carrying that baby, it didn't bother me at all that you ended up in the whorehouse. It was where you belonged."

"You made me think you loved me. You're disgusting, Dredger."

"I made you think a lot of things. Like I believed the boy was mine. He could have been, I guess, except for those brown eyes. No, those are Branigan eyes. They are exactly like your father's eyes, Branigan."

Dredger walked over to the edge of the cliff and

looked up the valley. He checked his watch again. "You were so useful to me up there, Annie, above the bar. What's the pastor saying? What's the deputy saying? What are the miners saying? You were a goldmine of information to me, honey."

Annie pulled Tommy closer to her.

"We all make choices, Annie. Choices to live, choices to survive. You made your own choices." Dredger shrugged. "But now you're leaving town. You and the boy won't be of any more use to me."

Alec moved his shoulder. Dredger's shot had cut just under his shoulder blade. The bleeding had stopped, and he knew he'd be all right.

Dredger turned to Alec. "Some sheriff you are. Letting yourself get shot like that."

"Why did you do it, Dredger?" Alec asked. "Why did you kill the teacher?"

"So you figured that out, did you?"

"Someone killed her husband while Branigan was in jail, and so it couldn't have been Branigan. And then the question was who else could have murdered both the teacher and her husband. He was heading out to your place to get the money that his wife had before she died."

"I didn't know she was married," Luc said.

"I suspected it was you, Dredger. I just couldn't figure out why." Alec eased himself away from the rock and took the locket out of his pocket. "Do you recognize this locket?"

"That's my wife's locket."

"You gave it to your wife. And who is the picture inside?"

"It's my sister, Laura."

"No, it isn't. It's Laura Wallace and this locket was hers, wasn't it?"

"So what if it was?"

"Laura Wallace and her whole family are dead. Neil McArthur recognized her picture. I bet Eileen recognized it, too."

Dredger looked hard at him. "So what if they're dead?"

"How did you come by Laura Wallace's locket? And her daddy's watch. You thought the Wallace family would be overlooked with everyone else who died during the Galveston hurricane, didn't you?"

"A lot of people died in that storm," Dredger answered.

"But their ranch hands found them dead before the storm. It was suspicious how you disappeared. You were lucky no one found you for this long."

"They were the first people I killed, Sheriff. But it was self-defense."

"Self-defense?"

"That's right. I grew up right beside the Wallace ranch. We had a little ranch, but the big outfits like Wallace, they didn't want our little spread cluttering up their range. Wallace and his men accused me of cattle rustling. They gave me two weeks to leave Texas or they would hang me.

"I waited for a week. It was a Friday night and

all of his men were in town. I said my goodbyes to my family. I went by Wallace's place and told him I wasn't a cattle rustler, but I was leaving anyway to keep my family safe. He thought he was a big shot. Said I was a liar and lucky to be alive.

"And then I shot him. Just like that. While he lay there dying, I went in the house and one by one, I shot his wife and all his children. Including Laura.

"Laura and I were the same age and we'd gone to school together." Dredger sounded regretful. "I always hoped we would end up together. I didn't want to kill her but she'd have the law on me. So I shot her.

"Wallace had this pocket watch." Dredger took the watch out of his vest. "He was so proud of this watch. I took it off him and I took the locket Laura was wearing, too. I went through the house and took all the cash and food I could find. Then I took his best horse and rode out of there."

"And no one ever found you?"

"The date was September 7, 1900. The next morning, the biggest hurricane that ever hit Galveston came rolling in. I kept riding north until I reached this place in the mountains. Home sweet home." He smiled.

"I never dreamt that someone from Texas would come up and find me here after ten years," Dredger concluded.

"But Eileen McArthur recognized you," Alec prodded.

"No, not at first. It turns out that Eileen McArthur was born Eileen Devlin. She was from Galveston and she remembered Laura Wallace because Laura was her teacher. I guess she recognized Laura's picture from her locket."

"Is that why you killed her?"

"I brought her up here one evening, to show her the view. She took exception when I tried to kiss her. The way she treated me, she certainly was suspicious about something. Then my wife's locket went missing. Eileen is the only one who could have taken it. So, I started asking her questions. One day, without thinking, she said that Laura Wallace was her favorite teacher. She said she had been shot. A few days after that I saw her with the locket. So I decided it was safer for me if she just disappeared."

"You killed her over a missing locket?" Alec asked.

"And she complained about that one little kiss to the pastor. I didn't want any trouble from her."

"Then her husband was killed," Alec said.

"Yeah, I killed her husband," Dredger admitted. "He came to me and told me he was Eileen McArthur's husband. He had a letter Eileen sent, telling him about finding the locket. He asked me about the Wallace family. He accused me of stealing his money from Eileen's trunk. He was going to be a problem."

"You have the biggest ranch around here," Annie said. "Why do you want this gold?"

"You can't ever have too much money, Annie. I learned that back in Texas. Besides, this is not Texas. Wallace thought he was driving me out, but I had every intention of returning. When I left Texas, I swore I would go back and set up there again. That's why I need the gold."

Alec was staring at him. "Still getting back at Wallace, after all these years."

Dredger looked at his watch again. "Time for the dynamite." He unfastened the watch from the chain on his vest.

"Here, Branigan, you can hold this for me." Dredger flung the watch at him. "I guess I've learned my lesson about taking jewelry from a dead man."

Dredger turned to face the boy. "Tommy, I want you to stay down here with your mama and the deputy. You need to keep them down here so they'll be safe."

"Watch them," Dredger said to Frank. The deputy trained his gun on the ground beside Alec.

The first blast came in a few minutes. The ledge shook and some rock fell from the face of the cliff, skittering around them as it fell into the valley below.

"We're going to die up here," Annie said. "And you're going to die with us, Frank. Do you think Dredger will leave anybody here alive?"

The deputy may not have been the sharpest nail in the box, but he must have figured Annie was right.

"Let's go," Frank said, and gestured with his gun up the cliff.

Annie tried to pull Branigan to his feet, but he could barely pull himself along.

Alec was a little better and Frank helped him up. Alec looked over at Annie. "I don't know which is safer, Annie, up there with Dredger and his guns, or down here on the ledge."

"Go, Sheriff. I'll stay here with Luc and Tommy."

. . . . .

Annie waited with Luc and Tommy. The second blast rocked the ledge even more, and then a huge mass of rock tumbled off the edge of the cliff, down around them.

The three of them edged along towards the cave at the farthest end of the ledge.

Rock from a third blast broke through the ledge and sent part of it crashing into the valley below. The path to the top of the cliff was obliterated.

"Tommy, let's go in the cave," Annie said. She eased Luc into the cave by gently lifting him under his arms and then supporting him as he hobbled along.

Inside the cave a torch still burned, and Annie could see empty dynamite boxes. She led Branigan to the very back of the cavern.

"You're a good woman, Annie."

"I missed you all these years, Luc. I was always so sorry about the way things turned out between us. So many regrets."

She turned to her son. "Tommy, there's something I need to tell you. This man here is your father."

"Is that what Dad meant when he said I had Branigan eyes?"

Annie never had a chance to answer. Another blast shook the cave around them. "I'm not sure coming in this cave was the best idea," she said. The next blast sent the roof of the cave falling around them.

Chapter Twenty-Four

Charlotte heard the first blast when she was crossing Bandit Creek down at the ford. She looked up the trail and she could see a mule train coming towards her. She ignored the mules and drove the car straight across the creek.

The second blast happened while she was driving up the road on the other side. The Oldsmobile had the power to climb the hill. She should have left the car where the trail snaked away from the road, but she pushed the gas pedal down as hard as she could. When the car wouldn't climb any farther, she turned it sideways on the trail and set the hand brake.

She heard the third blast while she was walking near the end of the trail. There at the top of the cliff, she could see Alec and his deputy. Dredger was fifty yards away setting off another blast.

The next minute, the entire side of the cliff tore away, plummeting to the valley below. Alec and his deputy dropped six feet down the other side of a deep chasm.

Charlotte felt the ground trembling under her feet. It felt like an earthquake. Dredger peered over the edge at the creek below. He looked around and saw Alec and his deputy. Dredger turned and raced towards his horse.

Charlotte crossed the top of the cliff, also towards the horse. Dredger reached it first and grabbed a shotgun. He turned to point it at Alec. Charlotte stopped behind Dredger.

He glanced at her. "I can't believe you're up here, too. How many people are sticking their nose in my business today?"

"I saw you shoot the sheriff."

"And I'm going to shoot him again." Charlotte was obviously no threat to him.

"Stop it. I have something to show you," she shouted.

He looked over his shoulder at her. "What's that girl?"

She'd taken her little revolver out of her purse. "This," she said, and she shot him. It took all seven of her bullets before he lay still.

But the ground kept moving. Suddenly, the whole cliff fell away from her feet. Dredger went with it.

· · · · ·

Beneath Luc Branigan, the ground rumbled like a freight train. He pulled Annie and the boy towards him. At least if they were going to die, they would be together. He held Tommy, and thought of his Branigan eyes.

· · · · ·

Charlotte ventured towards the new edge of the cliff and examined the debris. The rockslide had torn away the face of the mountain, sending it crashing down into the creek below. The mule train was below her. Most of the animals lay dead. A few men had run back up the trail and were now making their way back to the rubble of stone.

Alec and his deputy were nowhere to be seen. She'd seen Alec killed twice today. Once when Otto Dredger shot him, and then again in the rockslide. And she had lost him. Just like that.

She looked out over the edge again, looking for anything that moved. Maybe Alec was down there somewhere. She saw a black arm throwing some rocks away, reaching out from a crevice.

"Annie?" Charlotte called out. "Annie." A face looked up at her. "I'll get help," she shouted, relieved to be doing something, anything. She ran back from the cliff to the trail leading to Alec's car.

Running down to the car was a lot faster than the climb up. She got in and drove the twisting trail that led to the men below.

Beside the creek bed, two men were moving along the line of mules lying at the bottom of Deadman's Gap. If the mules were injured badly, they dispatched them with a single shot. The others they cut loose.

Charlotte got out of the car and pointed up to

Annie's face and arm sticking out of the wall of rock. "Do you think you can help her?"

The creek was backing up against the wall of rock that had plunged from the side of Crow Mountain. The two men waded into knee deep water to find some rope in the ruins of the mule train. Then they got into the car with Charlotte.

She drove them as high up as the car would take them. She let the two men go the rest of the way on their own. She was exhausted, and sat on the running board of the car to wait.

"Did I say you could drive my car up here?" a voice asked from the bush. "Didn't I tell you to go home?"

"Sheriff?" She stared at him, transfixed for a moment. "I thought you were dead." Her voice was a whisper. She stood up and ran to him. He wrapped his arms around her and she allowed herself to believe he was alive.

"I think you need to quit calling me Sheriff," he said. "If you're going to drive my car, I think you better start calling me Alec."

"You're always trying to tell me what to do," she said. "Shut up and kiss me."

. . . . .

Mrs. Miles was carrying one small suitcase when she got on the four o'clock train to Missoula. She walked down the aisle and found her husband. She settled into the seat beside him. The surprised look on his face broke her heart.

"I've decided to come with you," she said.

He obviously didn't know what to say. "Annie Hamilton gave me her ticket." Mrs. Miles took a deep breath and continued. "Just tell me one thing. What did she give you that I couldn't?"

· · · · ·

Sam Wilberforce walked to the front of the train to talk to the engineer. The mule train from the Ellis Mine hadn't arrived, but he didn't want to hold the train any longer. The creek had been backing up since early afternoon, and if he waited any longer, it looked like the track might flood.

Sam locked up the station and went home for dinner

· · · · ·

Luc Branigan and Annie Hamilton decided to leave town. Annie's past would never give them peace in Bandit Creek, and they needed a place to raise their son. Luc signed the ranch over to his brothers. Luc and Annie and Tommy left the next day on the four o'clock train to Missoula.

· · · · ·

The water in the creek continued to rise for the next three days. It was slow, but Bandit Creek gradually filled the creek bed and then broke over the banks.

That day on the mountain, Alec Forrest had managed to grab on to some bushes as the cliff thundered down into the valley. He never found Otto Dredger's body, and the deputy was missing as well.

By Monday, the sheriff moved his piano out of his house and into the teacherage up on the hill with Charlotte. If the creek continued to rise, they would have to move out of the teacherage as well.

"I can't be living with you like this," Alec said. "We'll scandalize everyone in town."

"It'll be a few days before anyone gets concerned," Charlotte said.

"We'll have to get married, Charlotte."

"I want to be a teacher."

"We'll work it out."

"And I want to ride astride."

"Anything else?"

"Well, I'd like to vote."

"You're a woman before your time, Charlotte."

Companion Books

Did you enjoy *Death at Bandit Creek*? Do you want to read more about Annie Hamilton? Don't miss:

The Ghost and Christie McFee
by Suzanne Stengl

And whatever happened to Eliza Dredger and her girls? Be sure to read:

A Bandit Creek Miracle
by Brenda Sinclair

Turn the page to read an excerpt from *The Ghost and Christie McFee*.

And following that, you can read the first chapter of *A Bandit Creek Miracle*.

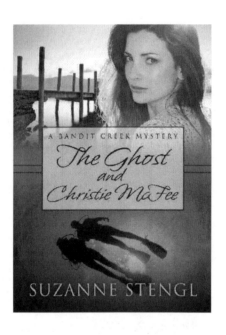

The Ghost and Christie McFee

by
Suzanne Stengl

(excerpt)

Charlie had anchored the boat so they'd enter the town from the northeast, as they usually did for this tour. The First Time Tour. Since Ripley and Terrence had done it several times, they knew their way through the trees to the starting point.

A few minutes later, the group reached the windmill that stood like a lone sentinel guarding the entrance to the Old Town. Its blades turned slightly in the lake currents. Nearby, another windmill had crashed to the ground, its blades half-buried in the silt.

Christie made a movement to swim up to the turning blades, but Gaven held her back. Surprising him, she pulled out of his grasp. He swam in front of her, motioned for her to look at him, and then pointed to his watch. She seemed to understand.

If she touched everything, they'd never finish the tour in the allotted time. He held out his hand and she took it. Together they floated over the half-buried windmill and reached the street sign that said Stokes Road. This sign really was authentic.

Ripley and Terrence hovered at either end of the sign, pointing to it. If the others remembered Charlie's talk, this was the part where he'd said they'd enter the town at Stokes Road—named after one of the early founders of Bandit Creek.

From there, they skimmed over the horse corrals and reached the end of Main Street. Tall and gloomy, the building fronts butted against each other. Boardwalks lined the street and the hitching posts stood strong and sturdy.

Much of the debris that had peppered the bottom of the lake had been gathered by the treasure hunters, but not all of it. As they journeyed past the stables, they saw some rusted buckets and a steel wagon wheel with five spokes. A few bottles with flat sides poked up out of the silt—clear glass, green glass, and even blue glass.

The volunteers had lined up many undamaged bottles and dishes on the shelves in the museum but, Gaven knew, there were also complete pieces inside the buildings.

They remained because the treasure hunters didn't care about old bottles and dishes. They searched for gold, not antiques, and that was a good thing. Otherwise the town would have been stripped long ago. At any rate, much of the town remained as it was on the days the floodwaters rose in late November of 1911.

Back then, there was mostly horse traffic, and horse and buggy. Only a few cars. Most of those cars had made it out in time. Some had not. Now the rusting cars and dilapidated buggies scattered along the street, resting in the places where the flood had deposited them, like the buckboard snugged against the hitching post in front of the Last Chance Saloon.

Next door, in front of the Blacksmith's Shop, a flatbed wagon had been abandoned with its load of barrels. Barrels without lids—pried off by the treasure hunters as they'd scavenged for the legendary gold.

The newlywed couple peered inside the Blacksmith's Shop, pausing at the entrance, hopefully remembering his instructions to stay outside. From where they floated, they'd be able to see the forge and the anvils and some of the abandoned tools, the hammers and vises.

Further down Main Street, Ripley and Terrence waited for the group, circling above the carriage that sat marooned in the middle of the road.

Christie jerked his hand, squeezing hard. Then she clutched his arm with both hands as she stared across the street at Maggie O'Connor's Boarding House.

Movement caught his eye, on the second floor . . . the faded checkered curtains fluttering in the light currents through the open window. She must have been paying attention to Charlie's ghost stories.

Taking hold of one of her hands, he held it in both of his, wanting to reassure her, and he waited for her to calm down again. When she realized what she'd seen was only curtains, she ducked her head. She must have been embarrassed. Pulling her hand away, she swam to where the newlyweds looked through the door of the Blacksmith's Shop.

She would be sufficiently spooked now to stay out of the buildings and he wouldn't worry about her going inside. The last thing he needed was one of his tourists getting their equipment tangled up inside a door or under a ceiling.

Outside of Maggie O'Connor's Boarding House, the older couple inspected the hanging sign over the boardwalk. A brightly painted piece of wood suspended from two thick chains off a beam above the door. It would have been easy to spot as travelers came up the street from the train station.

They continued toward the carriage where Ripley and Terrence pretended to drive. All along the street, the tall false fronts looked down on them, many with empty windows. Some of the windows wore shutters. Others held pieces of glass, probably broken when the floodwaters advanced.

As they floated past Garvey's Saloon, the half door swung faintly, like a patron had just entered.

Across from Garvey's, the building had a stoop attached to the front. Although the stoop leaned, the rest of the building stood tall and solid. A school of cutthroat trout flickered out the empty second story window.

By now, they'd caught up with Ripley and Terrence, and they all drifted past the newspaper office, called the *Bandit Creek Gazette* even then.

The signs on the buildings helped to tell the story of old Bandit Creek. Some of them were simple, and some were more elaborate. Like the one above the Powder Horn Saloon.

The Powder Horn had probably been the most popular drinking establishment of its day. It was the only saloon that had been recreated when Bandit Creek was rebuilt downstream.

The Men's Club, with its second floor balcony, stood next to the Powder Horn. From that balcony, a person could see much of what happened on the

Main Street of the town.

This was a part of the story Charlie loved to tell. The high class establishment boasted a Men's Club from the front but—from the back—it was a brothel.

As the stories went, this brothel's clientele consisted of wealthy men in town, and many of them lived in the mansions on the River Road. These mansions backed onto a lane, the same lane that ran behind the Main Street buildings.

The men could slip into the laneway behind their homes, cross over to the Men's Club, and climb the back stairs to the rooms used by the prostitutes. The fact that the Men's Club was a brothel was one of the worst kept secrets in Bandit Creek.

Gaven checked for Christie, and noticed she was staying close to the older couple. She was supposed to be with him, but she probably felt embarrassed about mistaking the waving curtains for a ghost. At least, she hadn't had to deal with—

As he had the thought, he was proved wrong. A huge white sheet burst out from the second floor balcony, causing the newlyweds, the older couple and Christie to tighten together in alarm.

Ripley and Terrence were up to their tricks again. They must have rigged the sheet like a sling shot. Now, the huge whiteness floated ominously above the street, and then slowly began to settle.

Ripley and Terrence swam to the side, out of the way.

As the puff of white floated down, the older couple looked at each other, shrugged and moved aside. The newlyweds nodded, looked at Ripley and Terrence and also got out of the way.

Only Christie hadn't figured it out yet. Dropping to the lake floor, she curled up in a ball.

Her first diving trip would be memorable.

Gaven pointed to the boys, they understood, and gathered up the sheet. He swam over to Christie and tried to get her attention, but she had her eyes squeezed shut. He tapped her hand. She flinched. Then he took her hand in his, hoping she would recognize his touch.

She did, opening those beautiful hazel green eyes. He pointed to the boys who were standing on their heads with the sheet bundled in their arms— the pose they used to suggest their unconcern. Any other time, it would have been funny, but at the moment he was worried about frightening a new diver. One who was already uneasy.

Letting herself rise from the bottom, she held on to his hand and watched the boys. Then, as if finally understanding it wasn't a ghost, she closed her eyes briefly, and pulled away from him.

Between the curtains and the sheet, it was too much.

Gaven decided he would have to do something about the boys. They loved the idea of ghosts in the Old Town, but he couldn't have them scaring a new diver.

With the commotion over, they traveled past the bank, past Mather & Son General Store, past Howard Massey's Harness Shop. And the Sheriff's Office and the jail and the Town Hall.

Finally they came to the Opera House—home of the famous singer, Jo-Jo Sullivan. Charlie's research said her voice was so beautiful she was called the Siren of Bandit Creek.

Last on the tour, they stopped at the Train Station where the divers could look inside the windows and see the telegraph office. They could float above the rusted tracks of the Montana Northern and see the graveyard beyond. But that was a tour for another day.

The newlywed woman had her camera out again, photographing her husband, with fins and arms crossed, as he leaned against the door to the telegraph office. The older couple hovered six feet higher, studying the sign above the door.

Ripley and Terrence sat in the Model T Ford parked out front, pretending to drive it. Charlie had told the group it was a 1908 five passenger touring car. An impressive vehicle back in the day. Not so impressive now, with its folded canvas roof in tatters, the strips of material moving in the slight current.

He looked around for Christie, thinking she might be interested in the car. But she wasn't up the street in front of the Opera House. She wasn't inside the telegraph office. She wasn't across the train tracks.

Not a sign of her. Not even a trail of exhaled air bubbles. Panic lumped in his throat.

A little rainbow trout wandered out of the second story window of the train station, crossed the tracks and disappeared in the direction of the graveyard.

You can find *The Ghost and Christie McFee* at your favorite online retailer site.

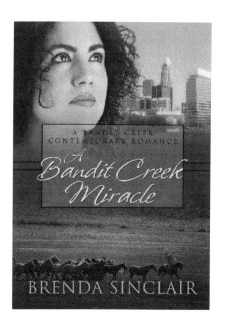

A Bandit Creek Miracle

by
Brenda Sinclair

(excerpt)

"Where is that damn hotel?"

Amanda Bailey steered her three-year-old red BMW coupe along the streets of Bandit Creek, Montana. The town's population hovered at around three thousand, and she'd convinced herself she could locate her destination without directions. She hadn't planned to arrive after dark.

Glancing at her watch, she discovered the time was already twenty minutes after ten. Thankfully, the highways were clear. But having driven almost non-stop from Helena, she couldn't wait for this day to end. Her eyes strained to focus on the road ahead, and she still hadn't spotted the New Golden Nugget Hotel.

She continued driving up one street and down another, convinced the hotel would appear around the next corner. As she spotted a diner, her stomach growled a reminder that she hadn't eaten since noon. Several pickup trucks and two cars were parked in front. Amanda pulled into a parking spot across the street from Ma's Kitchen.

"Well, Ma, I hope you serve up directions as well as meals." Amanda grabbed her purse off the passenger seat and clambered out of the car. She stretched her back, hunched and released her shoulders, and then inhaled the clean country air. There wasn't any familiar city noise. No ambulance sirens screaming, no horns honking. Except for a dog barking in the distance, the town remained eerily quiet.

Amanda dashed across the pavement, dodging a few puddles of snowy mush that threatened to ruin her new leather fashion boots. A tiny bell tinkled overhead as she entered the diner, and the aroma of strong coffee teased her nose. All conversation ceased, and a dozen heads swivelled toward the door to acknowledge the new arrival. Surprised expressions replaced the locals' welcoming smiles when they spotted her. Obviously, at this time of night, they'd expected to see a familiar face.

"Come in, dear." A plump woman with tight curly silver hair done up in a bun strode toward her carrying a menu. Her cheery floral apron covered a short-sleeved white blouse and neat navy slacks, a tea towel rode her right shoulder, and keen eyes peered at her from behind out-of-date eyeglasses.

"Hello. I'd kill for a cup of coffee." Amanda glanced around the diner. A horseshoe shaped counter with red-vinyl upholstered stools caught her eye. A row of booths sat against the far wall, and various square wooden tables and low-backed chairs utilized the remaining floor space. Flimsy red gingham curtains framed the front windows and a variety of historical photographs hung on the white painted walls. The term 'quaint' flashed through her mind. A perfect setting for a 1950's diner scene in a movie, she thought. Do the big-name California film producers know about this place?

"Often hear 'kill for a cup of coffee' first thing in the morning, not at this time of night." The woman chuckled and motioned Amanda forward. "We don't bother with a PLEASE WAIT TO BE SEATED sign like you see in the city. Just pick a seat and plant it, honey."

As Amanda cautiously stepped across the slush-spattered linoleum floor, she removed her black wool ¾-length coat revealing a white cashmere sweater tucked into black dress pants. She chose a table beside a window and slung her coat over the chair back. She lowered herself onto the seat, placed her purse on the table, and loosened the aqua cashmere scarf wrapped around her neck.

Her server set the menu in front of her and then stood hands on hips.

"Thanks, Ma." Amanda picked up the menu.

"Actually, honey, the name's Lucy. And that's George over there inside the horseshoe jawing with them cowboys." Lucy pointed in the gentlemen's direction with her thumb as if hitchhiking on the I-90. Hearing his name, George looked up and waved.

"Sorry, the sign outside…"

"Most newcomers to town make the same mistake. Usually, I don't even bother to correct the tourists." Lucy cackled and stuck out her beefy hand. "You must be the gal replacing the manager at the Ellis bank during her maternity leave. Catherine dropped by for lunch and mentioned you'd be arriving today."

"Amanda Bailey." She shook Lucy's slightly calloused hand. "Sorry, my hands feel like ice."

"As soon as the sun goes down seems the temperature takes a nose dive. I'll fetch you a mug of coffee to warm your insides and lift your spirits."

"Just black, please. Do you have decaf?" Amanda required something stronger than coffee to drag her out of this dark mood, but it didn't look like they served wine here.

She detested winter weather and she hated small towns. Her parents insisted she and her siblings spend summers with her grandparents at her mother's small Minnesota hometown. There was no movie theatre or even a library, and she soon discovered that her grandmother's sole source of entertainment was gossiping with her lady friends.

"Nope. None of them fancy lattes and such neither, just plain old coffee." Lucy turned and scurried away.

"Why am I not surprised?" muttered Amanda. Bandit Creek was the last place on earth she wanted to be. A city girl through-and-through, she'd attempted every means possible to avoid this small town purgatory. But her boss and best friend, Susan Sanders, warned her that if she expected a future promotion to manager of a city bank she should accept this temporary assignment.

She'd barely glanced at the menu before the server returned to the table and plunked down a white ceramic mug of steaming brew.

"Decided what you want?"

Amanda thought the woman appeared a-little-rough-around-the-edges. But a rough edge here and there never hurt anyone.

"I'll have a bowl of the homemade chicken noodle soup, a cheeseburger, loaded, and sweet potato fries, please." Amanda passed the menu back to Lucy. "Does salad come with the burger?"

"Yep, coleslaw comes with your meal."

"I'm sorry, but I don't consider coleslaw to be salad," stated Amanda, smiling. She caught a glimpse of one of the guys seated at the horseshoe counter. The Hollywood-handsome cowboy faced backwards on the stool, slouching, resting his elbows on the counter behind him. He smiled broadly and his big brown eyes met hers for several seconds causing her heartbeat to race. Thankfully, the waitress had seated her before she'd fallen weak-kneed under the spell of this good-looking cowboy. After the horrendous year she'd just endured, Amanda enjoyed the attention he bestowed on her.

"Close enough. We put two kinds of cabbage in it – green and red." Lucy tapped her pen on the order pad. "So that's soup, cheeseburger, sweet tater fries and coleslaw. You're my kind of gal. Healthy appetite."

Amanda grimaced at the comment. She still struggled to maintain her weight, having lost so many pounds during the year-long chemo and radiation treatments and recovery. All of her girlfriends back in Helena envied her ability to eat everything in sight, one consolation for surviving the cancer. She leaned her elbows on the table, tented her fingers. "I might be tempted to order a piece of lemon pie."

"There's one piece of lemon meringue left. Those cowboys dropped by after the cattlemen's meeting for coffee and pie. And the other folks arrived when the movie theatre let out." Lucy whispered in a conspirator-like manner, "I'll hide that last piece under the counter until you finish the first course."

"I wondered why there were so many people in here at this hour. Thank you for saving the pie." Amanda smiled. Dessert always cheered her up. "Where's the Ladies' Room?"

Lucy pointed toward the overhead sign in back and then headed toward the kitchen.

Amanda blew on the steaming coffee, took a sip, and then glanced toward the horseshoe counter. The cowboy met her eyes again, and his bushy moustache twitched slightly as his full lips hinted at a grin. She'd spent most of the past year bald, her head covered with a scarf, nauseous and weak as a kitten. Being admired by a handsome cowboy brightened Amanda's mood a notch and ignited her playful side. She copied his position: slouching in her chair, crossing her ankles and arms, staring right back at him. His grin broadened.

A minute later, Amanda regretted her playfulness, her body aching from sitting in a fixed position while driving for so many hours. Her leg muscles screamed 'what the hell are you doing'? And she fervently prayed she didn't slide off the edge of the chair and land on her butt under the table. Feeling her face redden, she struggled to stand, grabbed her purse, and headed toward the restrooms in back.

As she wended her way between the tables, she observed the other patrons. A gray-haired couple occupied a corner booth, and they smiled as she glanced in their direction. The cowboys seated around the horseshoe nodded and touched the brim of their Stetsons as she approached. One fellow appeared older than the others, but none of them stood out as anything other than typical small town guys. Mr. Hollywood-handsome being the exception.

"Evening, ma'am." The handsome cowboy's deep masculine voice rumbled in his broad chest, and he removed the Stetson and set it on his thigh. He wore jeans, a chambray shirt, open denim jacket and well-worn cowboy boots which suggested he was the genuine article.

"Good evening." Amanda stopped directly in front of the good-looking fellow.

"I wasn't eavesdropping, but I couldn't help overhear your conversation with Lucy. So, you're the gal replacing my sister-in-law, Catherine." The cowboy leaned forward, extended his hand. "Jeremy Branigan."

"Please to meet you, Mr. Branigan. I'm Amanda Bailey." Amanda shook his hand and felt an electric current race up her arm. She'd never felt such an immediate attraction to a guy before, and she imagined running her fingers through his dark brown, almost shoulder-length curls. The laugh lines around his eyes hinted at his sense of humor, and she'd always been attracted to a deep male voice that rattled her mind in equal proportion to the degree of rattling in the fellow's chest.

Jeremy introduced her to the other gentlemen seated around the horseshoe, and Amanda shook their hands. She'd never remember them all, but the name Jeremy Branigan was permanently burned into her mind like a brand on a steer's hide.

They just stared at each other for an embarrassing length of time. Amanda cleared her throat and shifted to her other foot. Her brain had dissolved into mush, and she couldn't think of one intelligent thing to say. Those beautiful brown eyes almost spoke to her when he smiled. She mentally shook herself, fearing she might melt into a puddle at his feet.

"I guess I'll be seeing you around town, ma'am." Jeremy replaced his Stetson on his head, touched the brim.

Amanda exhaled, unaware she'd been holding her breath while she watched the cowboy slide his long legs back under the counter. She stumbled down the narrow hallway toward a door labelled LADIES while mentally restarting her thought processes.

She glanced back toward the horseshoe counter and caught Jeremy watching her. Had the handsome cowboy felt a similar attraction to her? Or like most guys did he just habitually check out a woman's behind? She hoped Jeremy hadn't been disappointed. She dashed into the Ladies' room and locked the door, admitting to herself she couldn't fault Jeremy's behavior. She'd been guilty of checking out a few male rear ends on the sly, too.

On her way back to the table, a pleasantly-plump, casually dressed couple waved her over to their table.

"I bet you're the new banker. I could tell right off, you being all dressed up so professional and all." The fellow was obviously expecting her to confirm his guess.

"Amanda Bailey." Introductions were made and hands were shook. She assumed they were customers at the bank.

By the time she returned to her table, the cowboys had left the diner.

Lucy arrived with her soup, and Amanda suddenly remembered she required directions to the hotel. The friendly woman's banter and the testosterone-oozing cowboy had distracted her from her second purpose in stopping.

"Before I forget, Lucy, could you please give me directions to the New Golden Nugget Hotel?" Amanda reached for the soup spoon.

"Yep. I'll draw you a map, honey." Lucy grabbed a paper napkin out of the holder and dug out a ballpoint pen from her apron pocket. "You'll love staying at the Nugget. After the flood in 1911, Mr. and Mrs. Vanderberg rebuilt the hotel. Their great granddaughter, Elsie Rhodes, owns the place now.

She's a tad eccentric, but she's a good soul."

Amanda studied the completed map. The combination of lines and squiggles resembled an aerial view of a corn maze in August. The street names were indecipherable. Doctors wrote more legibly. "Could you please explain the route, too?" Amanda memorized the directions as recited.

When she asked for her bill, Lucy informed her that Jeremy Branigan paid for her meal. Amanda started to object, but Lucy waved off her protests. "Don't worry about it, honey. That wealthy rascal carries around hundred dollar bills for pocket change."

&

You can find *A Bandit Creek Miracle* at your favorite online retailer site.

About the Author

Amy Jo Fleming writes romantic suspense and she loves a story that leaves you wondering about the characters after you read the final page. Amy Jo has always been a writer. In university, she wrote poetry when she should have been studying. She loves to read a good mystery or legal thriller.

In another life, Amy Jo was a lawyer. Now she is a freelance writer. Amy Jo loves to hike all over the world, from Calgary to Australia, and from Scotland to Spain. Her favorite place to hike is in the Rocky Mountains just a few miles up the road from her home.

She lives in Calgary with her husband David (an engineer) and their dog, Abbie.

www.AmyJoFleming.com

@AmyJoFlemingLLB

Find more books by Amy Jo Fleming at
www.AmyJoFleming.com

&

If you enjoyed *Death at Bandit Creek*
you can help others find this story
by leaving a short review at
your favorite online retailer site.

Made in the USA
Columbia, SC
20 June 2018